"I actually own this nightmare,"

Zachary said softly to himself as he watched the blonde from the concession stand rounding up the dozen or so cows that had wandered into the drive-in's lot.

Within a few minutes she'd led them out and returned, smiling broadly. "A three-piece suit. Wild!" she exclaimed. "You know, for a moment there I didn't know what seemed more out of place, Old Lady Harrison's herd or that suit."

"I want to see your manager," Zachary said slowly. *"Now!"*

Sharon spread her arms wide and grinned. "Your wish is my command, sir. One manager, at your service." She held out her right hand. "Sharon Wheeler, manager of Wheeler's Drive-In, oldest operating outdoor theater in America. And you're—?"

"Zachary St. Clair, owner of St. Clair Theater Corporation—and your boss," he replied, his dark eyes narrowing into threatening slits.

"And I'm dead," Sharon whispered under her breath, closing her eyes.

"Not yet, Miss Wheeler," Zachary replied tersely. "But I'm beginning to believe it could be arranged."

Dear Reader:

The spirit of the Silhouette Romance Homecoming Celebration lives on as each month we bring you six books by continuing stars!

And we have a galaxy of stars planned for 1988. In the coming months, we're publishing romances by many of your favorite authors such as Annette Broadrick, Sondra Stanford and Brittany Young. Beginning in January, Debbie Macomber has written a trilogy designed to cure any midwinter blues. And that's not all—during the summer, Diana Palmer presents her most engaging heroes and heroines in a trilogy that will be sure to capture your heart.

Your response to these authors and other authors of Silhouette Romances has served as a touchstone for us, and we're pleased to bring you more books with Silhouette's distinctive medley of charm, wit and—above all—romance.

I hope you enjoy this book and the many stories to come. Come home to romance—for always!

Sincerely,

Tara Hughes
Senior Editor
Silhouette Books

KASEY MICHAELS

Popcorn
and Kisses

Silhouette Romance

Published by Silhouette Books New York

America's Publisher of Contemporary Romance

To Eleanor Durkin...
>I can scarcely bid you good-bye,
>even in a letter.
>I always made an awkward bow.
>God bless you!

>(John Keats, 1820)

...To me you shall always be forever young.

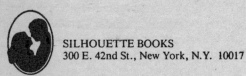

SILHOUETTE BOOKS
300 E. 42nd St., New York, N.Y. 10017

Copyright © 1988 by Kathie Seidick

ISBN: 0-373-08572-9

First Silhouette Books printing April 1988

America's Publisher of Contemporary Romance

Printed in the U.S.A.

Books by Kasey Michaels

Silhouette Romance

Maggie's Miscellany #331
Compliments of the Groom #542
Popcorn and Kisses #572

KASEY MICHAELS

considers herself a late bloomer, having written her first romance novel after devoting seventeen years to her husband, four children, the little league and the avoidance of housework. Author of five Regency novels, she has also published a nonfiction book about her son's kidney transplant under her own name, Kathryn Seidick.

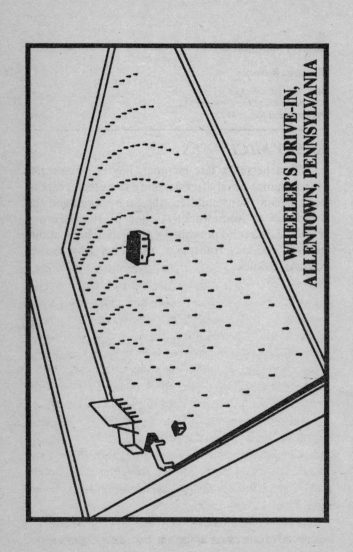

WHEELER'S DRIVE-IN,
ALLENTOWN, PENNSYLVANIA

Chapter One

The old-fashioned clock face projected onto the wide, curved screen showed the seconds slowly ticking away. The clock was surrounded on all sides by a host of cartoon popcorn boxes, hot dogs, candy bars and soda cups. Each character was equipped with stick-figure legs and arms and all were merrily dancing to the beat of a familiar-sounding syncopated tune.

As the single hand on the clock reached twelve, the large number six that had been displayed in the center of the dial disappeared and was replaced by an equally large number five. The music was momentarily muted as a voice announced: "Five minutes, folks! Just five minutes till show time. There's still time to visit our snack bar before our feature presentation of the evening. Five minutes to show time."

The clock hand had already begun another circuit before the music came up again, but the sprightly red-

and-white-striped popcorn chorus girls in their high
spiked heels, the cane-carrying, top-hat-clad hot dogs,
the brightly wrapped candies and the foam-topped
fizzing soda cups never missed a beat.

The crowd at the snack bar was smaller now, as
most of the patrons at Wheeler's Drive-In Theater
had already stocked up on the goodies they believed
necessary to get them through the second feature
without fear of starvation, and the usual long lines
that extended outside the rest room doors had already disappeared. Parents hustled their pajama-clad
youngsters back to their cars before the lights inside
the snack bar were dimmed and they had to make their
way along the gravel paths in the dark.

"Three minutes, folks! Three minutes till show
time. There's still time to visit our snack bar. Three
minutes till show time," the faceless voice droned out,
and a few harassed mothers were forced to physically
remove their balky toddlers from the playground located directly beneath the movie screen, promising
that the movie they were about to see was much more
fun than the swings, the sliding board or the old-
fashioned foot-powered merry-go-round.

There was one section of the drive-in that seemed to
escape the hustle and bustle of the between-shows intermission, and that was the area that made up the
shadowy last three rows of the outdoor theater. Here
there were no station wagons loaded with sleeping bags
and jugs of homemade lemonade. No lawn chairs were
set up outside the cars, which tended to be mostly
older sports cars, pickup trucks or supercompacts.

There were speakers in the back rows, two on each of the metal poles that lined the built-up parking ramps between the small roadways, but many of them were never turned up or hung on an open side window so that the movie could be heard as well as seen. No matter what story lines were being projected, from lighthearted comedies to action-adventure thrillers, for the patrons in the secluded back rows the subject was always the same—romance.

It was springtime, and just one more night in the seemingly endless string of nights when Wheeler's Drive-In attracted moviegoers with its double features, cartoon specials and homey atmosphere amid the softly rolling hills just outside of Allentown, Pennsylvania.

At last the ticking clock disappeared, and the feature presentation, a parental-guidance-suggested spy spoof, appeared on the screen. The lights on the snack bar roof went out, and soon the only sounds to be heard other than the actors' voices were the occasional outbursts from cranky children fighting for equal space in the back seat, and a few inadvertent horn honkings as the moviegoers struggled to balance their popcorn and get comfortable at the same time.

The door to the dark projection booth opened and closed. "A pretty full house for our first Thursday night of the season, considering that it looked like rain earlier, don't you think, George?" the feminine voice asked above the whir of the projector.

George Blakeman, head—and only—projectionist at Wheeler's for more than forty-five years, only grunted, busy with the job at hand, loading the second reel onto the forty-year-old number-two projector that he had dubbed Veronica Lake. Number one had been christened with the name Gloria Swanson and would run out of film right after the scene in the Turkish bath that was already on-screen.

"Can you believe they actually get paid to write this junk?" he asked, shaking his balding head in disgust. "This guy's walking around in all that steam with nothing on but a towel, and when the bad guys show up he calmly reaches behind his back and pulls out a damn *machine gun* to blow them all away. I didn't see any bulges under that towel. Now where do you suppose he had that gun—taped to his rosy butt?"

Sharon Wheeler smiled at her friend's criticism of one of the previous winter's top-grossing movies—for Wheeler's was a second run theater—and pulled herself up to sit atop the large, scarred wooden worktable, her sneakers lazily swinging back and forth a good distance above the floor. "What else could he do, George? Snap them silly with a rolled-up Turkish towel? Besides, if he'd done that they'd have lost their PG rating. Just be glad we could get the film before it came out on home videotape. We need a couple more crowds like this one to make back what we lost on those three rainy nights last weekend."

George watched through the small square paneless window of the concrete-block projection booth for the flashing white circle to appear in the corner of the screen, a cue that would alert him to switch on the second projector. Seeing the quick flash, he hit the button, waited for a second signal, then shut off the first projector so he could load the third reel.

"How's the cash box doing, Shari?" he asked, still not looking at his young boss, whom he had known since she was born. "Is the snack bar holding its own?"

Sharon's pert, freckle-dusted nose crinkled a bit as she added and subtracted some figures in her head. "The steak sandwiches sold out already, but since the price of the meat went up, I'd say we won't pick up anything extra there. I think I can up our price a quarter, but I can't make it too high or we'll scare the customers away. The ice cream went well, too, probably because it's been so darn hot outside."

As if to prove her point about the heat, Sharon undid the last two buttons on her blouse, then tied the two sides together under her breasts, baring her midriff. Her tanned legs, highly visible beneath the cutoff denim shorts, continued to swing back and forth, trying in vain to create some small breeze in the airless projection room. "We've got to get the air conditioner in here fixed tomorrow, before the weekend. It can't be good for the film to be in so much heat."

"It's not exactly great for the projectionist either, Shari," George pointed out gruffly, wiping his shiny forehead with a big red printed handkerchief. "Maybe the new owner will spring for a new air conditioner. This one's nearly as old as I am."

Sharon ran her hands through both sides of her shoulder-length honey-blond hair, tucking the heavy strands back behind her ears. "Dreaming again, George?" she asked, lightly hopping down from her perch. "Wheeler's has had two owners since Popsie died, and neither of them spent so much as a cent on the place. We may be the oldest operating drive-in theater in America, but to our esteemed owners we were only a tax write-off to balance out the companies' indoor theaters downtown and in the malls. What makes you think this St. Clair Theater Corporation is going to be any different?''

George carefully replaced the rewound reel in its case, slid the case into its proper slot in the numbered reel storage bin located under the worktable, then shrugged his shoulders hopefully. ''The St. Clair bunch picked us up for next to nothing when it bought the indoor theaters from Hardesty Features. The way I figure it, it's not like it would break them to throw a little of the green stuff in our general direction. Right?''

Sharon started for the door, knowing she had to get back to the snack bar to supervise the six high school girls she had hired as summer help, but she turned back for a moment to seek some more assurance from her old friend. ''You don't think they'll decide to turn Wheeler's into an X-rated theater, do you, George? I mean, companies are doing a lot of that sort of thing in some areas—although I don't think St. Clair's has any of them.''

''It's anybody's guess, Shari,'' he answered, wishing he could say something to allay her fears. ''But, hey, if they do, you won't have to worry your pretty head anymore about replacing the playground equipment. The whole place will be one big playground— and no kids allowed. It's a good thing the cows in Old Lady Harrison's field next door don't know how to use binoculars. Right?''

Sharon shook her head and turned away. "Thanks, George, for those stirring, truly inspiring words. You've been a big help. If I'm ever stuck at the bottom of a well I know I can count on you to toss me down a bucket of water."

"Hey," he called after her as she opened the door, "don't go away mad. I was just making a joke. St. Clair doesn't have any X-rated theaters, Shari, I checked. Just stop worrying that pretty head of yours until somebody from the company shows up to inspect the place. After all, there's nothing you can do about it anyway. Right?"

Relenting, Sharon's mouth formed a small smile as she nodded her agreement. "Like you say, George, we'll just have to wait and see. I guess it's just that I love this place so much—" As she heard the tremor come into her voice she shook her head as if to banish her darker thoughts. "Oh, well. I've got to get back to work. And tomorrow is Friday—we should get an even bigger crowd. I'll send one of the girls in soon with your usual, okay?"

George licked his lips with exaggerated fervor at the mention of his nightly snack of two hot dogs barely visible beneath mounds of ketchup, mustard and Sharon's secret sauce. "Send them in when our hero turns his motorbike into a rocket launcher and wipes out enemy headquarters. That'll give me plenty of time to eat before the next reel change. Oh, yeah, and I wouldn't say no to a couple of those nachos—just hold the jalapeño peppers. Right?"

"You got it," Sharon promised. Then she added thoughtfully, "You know, George, after watching *Spy in the Eye* seven times in three days, X-rated films don't sound so bad."

Sharon sighed before slipping out the door.

Zachary St. Clair had spent the better part of his Friday driving around Allentown and some of its nearby suburbs, cursorily examining the St. Clair Theater Corporation's latest acquisitions. So far, he was satisfied. The two shopping mall theaters, each comprised of six screen houses, were fairly new, strategically located and economically sound investments.

The three downtown theaters, two in Allentown and one in nearby Bethlehem, were older, and Zachary had already jotted down some notes concerning the feasibility of converting at least two of them into multiscreen houses.

But as pleased as he was with his findings, he was weary, having driven to Southeastern Pennsylvania from New York City that morning, and was beginning to regret his decision to inspect the last theater, Wheeler's—a drive-in of all things—before calling it a day and returning to his hotel.

He had already been on the road an hour, driving in circles as the daylight turned to dusk, trying to locate the rural theater that was advertised as being just fifteen minutes from center-city Allentown, and his never placid temper was beginning to surface with a vengeance. It had become a challenge, finding the theater, and now he was determined to ferret it out no matter how long it took.

This was the third time he had passed the same country inn, he was sure of it, and he decided the moment had come to throw in the towel and ask for directions. Pulling into the parking lot that fronted on the rural highway, he was just about to swing the car around when he saw the sign out of the corner of his eye.

"Wheeler's Drive-In Theater, Oldest Operating Drive-In in America" was spelled out in faded paint on the weather-beaten wooden sign that was lit by one small spotlight. Spying out a narrow-topped road just to the right of the inn, Zachary steered his sports car in that direction, cursing succinctly under his breath at the stupidity of placing a sign thirty feet back from the edge of the highway.

As he rounded a slight turn his headlights picked up the huge vintage black-backed outdoor screen that perched atop a heavy cross-beamed wooden base. "I feel like I've just entered the Twilight Zone," he muttered under his breath as he stopped the car beside a small wooden shed that served as the ticket office.

"Hi there! Neat car," the gangly, red-haired youth said cheerfully after blowing a shiny pink bubble, drawing it into his widely opened mouth and biting down so the bubble burst with a large pop. Then, maneuvering the huge wad of gum to one side so that his cheek had to stretch around it, the boy continued, "You're just in time for the cartoon if you hurry. We've got Woody Woodpecker this week. You alone? No kids in the back?" He leaned out of the shed and peered into the empty back seat. "We give lollipops, you know."

"Bully for you. One, please," Zachary said shortly, then looked down at his hand, amazed to see change from the five dollar bill he had passed over to the boy.

"Come to see *Spy in the Eye*, huh? Saw it three times myself. Great picture! All alone, huh? You know the first feature is a Disney?" The boy looked warily at Zachary, as if wondering just what was wrong with the guy that he'd come to a drive-in on his own.

Zachary didn't answer. He just pocketed his change, pushed the button that raised the darkly tinted side window to shut off any further conversation and stepped on the gas.

"Hey, mister—shut off your headlights! Only parking lights from this point. Can't you read the sign?" the boy yelled after the departing car before turning to greet a station wagon holding two adults and a small army of pajama-clad children.

Zachary chose a spot about six rows back from the screen and pulled in, hearing the bottom of his sports car scrape against the loose gravel as it moved over the rounded hump that angled the front of the car higher than the rear, giving a better view of the screen.

He lowered his window to reach for the speaker, only to find that he had parked too far away for the cord to reach inside the car. "I needed this," he growled softly, restarting the engine to pull back and move closer. The undercarriage scraped again, bringing a short, satisfying curse to his lips. It took two backups, and five more scrapes, to finally pull the car in at the correct angle, but once the speaker was hooked over the open window Zachary discovered that the sound didn't work.

"I should have known," he said ruefully, replacing the useless box on its stand, for he really hadn't come to see the movie anyway. Turning front, he looked toward the screen and saw dancing beams of light chasing one another around the white surface. "What the hell?" he mused, looking around at the other cars until he understood that several of the patrons had spotlights attached to their cars and were passing the time playing tag with one another on the blank screen.

He decided to take a closer look around before the movie started, and opened his door—just to hear it slam against the speaker post, dislodging the speaker, which then bounced against the fiberglass car door before falling to the ground. "Damn!" This wasn't getting any better.

Pulling the door shut, he angled his six-foot-four-inch frame around the floor-mounted gearshift and twisted himself onto the other bucket seat before nearly falling out of the passenger door as his left leg went into a cramp.

Limping slightly, and madder than he'd been since the day his golf cart had lost its brakes and landed him waist-deep in a water hazard on the third hole three years earlier, Zachary made for the front of the theater to inspect the screen up close.

He stopped dead, though, as he passed the first row, unable to believe what he was seeing. There, at the base of the screen, and enclosed by a sorry, sagging wooden fence, was the poorest excuse for a playground in the history of the world.

Ancient metal play equipment, all painted an uninspired slate-gray, was scattered willy-nilly over a large patch of weeds mixed with even larger patches of packed-down dirt. Two park benches placed together at one end of the playground were all the seating provided for the many mothers who were watching their children as they climbed and swung and whirled round and round on a huge flat metal circle, hanging on to the contraption's projecting metal arms for dear life as they screamed in glee.

"The liability insurance for this death trap has to be enough to choke a horse," he muttered under his breath before lifting his head to peer intently at the screen, checking on its condition. After only a moment, he shook his head, mouthed a short, unlovely word and turned on his heel, having seen enough—more than enough.

Car horns began to blow as the night grew darker and, in the customers' opinion, it was show time. The discordant sounds followed Zachary as he picked his way carefully back across the humps that made up the parking ramps and the pothole-pitted gravel paths separating them.

He headed straight to the low, white cement-block building that housed the snack bar and projection booth. The aroma of hot buttered popcorn, a smell he was used to, mingled incongruously with those of hot dogs, onions, frying steak and, of all things, sauerkraut.

As he stepped through one of the opened doorways into the brightly lit snack bar he nearly collided with a chubby, pajama-dressed, giggling toddler clutching an overflowing box of popcorn, who was running full tilt for the door, her older brother in hot pursuit, yelling, "You hafta *share*! Mom said so! *I'm telling!*"

Once completely inside, Zachary stood with his back against the wall and watched as seven young women raced back and forth across the open area behind the counters, which spanned the width of the room facing each of the two doorways, taking and filling huge orders without benefit of written bills or adding machines.

The smallest woman, a petite pony-tailed blonde, was dressed in an oversize red T-shirt, which had Wheeler's printed in large white letters on the back, and a pair of very short white shorts. She seemed to move up and down the length of the counter with the speed of light, filling orders and making change from a wide, three-pocket canvas belt she wore loosely tied around her waist, and never missing a beat—all accomplished while smiling at all the customers and winking at all the children.

Zachary shook his head yet again. He wasn't against hiring teenagers—all the St. Clair theaters hired teenagers—and the young women seemed pleasant and efficient enough, but how could the manager let them get away with dressing like that? Where were their uniforms, their aprons, their caps? Sloppy, slipshod management, he concluded. Damned sloppy.

Walking around to the front of the building, he located the door to the projection room and turned the handle. Locked. Well, he thought ruefully, that's something. At least the projectionist must have something on the ball. He raised his hand and rapped sharply on the door.

"Bathrooms on the other side," a male voice bellowed. "Can't you people read?"

"I'd like to speak with you for a moment," Zachary called loudly through the door, for the cartoon had begun and the snack bar speaker was located just above his head.

"I gave at the office," the voice yelled back. "Get lost!"

"I said open this door!" Zachary bellowed, almost glad to have an excuse to yell.

"Take a hike!"

"Now listen, buster—"

Zachary never finished the sentence. He was instead distracted by the sound of a high-pitched female scream, and he ran toward the snack bar to see who was getting killed and by whom. Rounding the corner he abruptly stopped in his tracks, having come face-to-face with, of all things, a large, brown-eyed cow.

"What the bloody hell—" he exploded, stepping back a pace.

"Moo-o-o-o," the cow responded, starting to move toward him, the heavy metal bell hanging from around her neck clang-clanging as the animal rocked her large brown and white head from side to side, her massive jaw working as she chewed her cud.

"Help me! Help me! That wild bull is trying to trample me!" pleaded a woman clad in a pink cabbage-rose-flowered cotton robe, fuzzy blue slippers and two dozen purple plastic hair rollers, as she convulsively grabbed Zachary by the arm.

Zachary might have been a city boy, but he knew damn well that the gentle-eyed bovine in front of him was no bull. "Calm down, lady," he snapped unsympathetically. "It's just an ordinary, everyday cow. Go back to your car, it's perfectly safe."

"No it isn't," she contradicted shrilly, still hanging on to Zachary's arm, her hot dog squashed in her fist, dripping catsup. "There's a whole herd of them stampeding through here." She disengaged one arm to point in the direction of the eighth row. "Look at all of them! Oh, my poor babies. They're all alone in the car. I only wanted a hot dog. What will I do?"

Suddenly the blonde from the snack bar appeared around the corner, a yardstick clasped in her right hand, a big red apple in her left. "I thought as much. Here we go again," she sighed, eyeing up the cow. "Hello there, Gertrude. So, how's tricks?"

When the cow only continued to chew, the young woman turned to the lady and smiled. "Go inside the snack bar, ma'am, and one of the girls will escort you safely back to your car," she said calmly, giving the woman a gentle push toward the corner. "There's nothing to worry about, I promise. You just make sure the girl gives you a free car pass you may use any time this season." Then, looking at the unappetizing lump squished tightly in the woman's right hand, she grimaced slightly and added, "And tell her to throw in another hot dog for you while she's at it, okay?"

"A free pass? For our whole car?" the woman repeated, lifting up her head so sharply that the curlers in her hair seemed to be reacting like finely tuned antennae. "Oh, aren't you nice! But—but, what about the cows? Where did they come from?"

"The fence must have broken down between the theater and Mrs. Harrison's pasture again, and her cows decided to try out our snack bar. You go on along now and I'll—um—I'll try to make like a shepherd and get the flock out of here." She lifted her hands to show the yardstick and apple as if to display just how she would go about rounding up the strays. "Come on, Gertrude, my dear, it's time you and your lady friends called it an evening," she said, patting the cow affectionately on her wide forehead as if to prove how totally harmless the animal was.

The lady reluctantly released Zachary's arm without bothering to thank him, and sprinted for the safety of the snack bar. The blonde, he noticed after inspecting his sleeve for creases, had already set off in the other direction, yardstick raised above her head as she held the apple out behind her like bait. Gertrude followed along behind her like a well-behaved house pet.

One hand to his mouth, Zachary watched as the young woman skillfully rounded up the dozen or so animals and paraded them down the path toward the far end of the theater lot while a loud woodpecker laugh echoed from the many speakers. As the strange procession passed by, patrons blew their horns or blinked their headlights on and off, and the girl alternately waved an imaginary hat in the air and executed exaggerated low bows in acknowledgment of their strange applause.

"I . . . own . . . this," Zachary said out loud slowly, unable to believe anything that had happened from the moment he had left the highway. "I actually *own* this nightmare."

Within a few minutes the blonde was back, minus the apple and the cows. She walked right up to him, smiling broadly, and placing her hands on her hips said, "A three-piece suit. Wild! You know, for a moment there I didn't know what seemed more out of place, Old Lady Harrison's herd or that suit. Anyway, thanks so much for letting that absurd woman latch on to you like that. My name's Sharon, by the way. If you'll wait here a moment I'll see if I can dig up a couple of free passes for you for your trouble."

She had already started to move away when Zachary fairly spit, "I don't want one of your free passes— or, for that matter, any of your free hot dogs—after all, it's not as if anyone in their right mind would be so foolish as to come here twice."

Walking back to him, still smiling, she offered, "All right. No passes for the man in his right mind. But how about a Wheeler special steak sandwich before you ride off into the sunset? You'll love it. Grilled paper-thin sliced steak served on a steamed roll and topped with cooked onions, sauce, pickles and hot peppers—pure ambrosia! It's the least I can do."

"You can skip the sales pitch, miss. Let's go inside. I want to see your manager," Zachary informed her, his voice hard.

Sharon's smile finally faded, and she winced slightly as she looked up into his grim face. "It's Sharon, remember? Oh, dear, you're not going to make a mountain out of this little molehill, are you, sir? After all, if you think about it for a while, the whole thing was really rather funny.''

"You'll notice that I'm not laughing."

Wrinkling up her nose, Sharon answered dully, "Yeah. Actually, I'd already noticed that, sir. Very well, follow me. I guess it might be better to go inside." Once again she turned and headed for the snack bar. "It *is* a lot cooler out here, you know. Don't you think—"

"*Damn it!* Woman, would you please move!"

"Whoops! Sorry about that, sir," she ended lamely, turning to look up at the man, who had collided with her as she had stopped without warning to take one last stab at placating him. "We'll go inside, right?"

Zachary was busy rubbing his chin, the part of his anatomy that had so lately met up with the top of Sharon's head. "You're very astute," he bit out angrily.

"I'm really sorry, sir," she said hurriedly. "It's just that I thought, well, it's such a lovely night, and it would be much more pleasant if we could—"

"I want to see your manager. Now!"

As if trying to put a bright face on it, Sharon spread her arms wide and grinned. "Your wish is my command, sir. One manager, at your service." Shifting the yardstick to her left hand, she held out her right hand and said, "Sharon Wheeler, manager of Wheeler's Drive-In, oldest operating outdoor theater in America. And you're—"

Zachary stared at the small hand for a long moment before taking it in his large one which nearly swallowed it as he gave it a firm shake, then held on. "Zachary St. Clair, owner of St. Clair Theater Corporation—and your boss," he replied, his dark eyes narrowing into dangerous slits.

"And I'm dead," Sharon whispered under her breath, closing her eyes.

"Not yet, Miss Wheeler," Zachary, overhearing, replied tersely. "But I'm beginning to believe it could be arranged."

Chapter Two

He's rather good-looking—for a fire-breathing monster, that is, Sharon thought as she reluctantly preceded Zachary St. Clair into the snack bar. But then, she thought as a small smile tugged at the corners of her mouth, Beelzebub had also supposedly been rather handsome, if one overlooked the horns and tail!

The lights inside the snack bar were dimmed, the girls inside the enclosure scurrying here and there, replenishing the supply of hot dogs on the carousel griller, loading freshly popped corn into the standby holding compartment and restocking the candy shelves; but it was neither dark enough nor hectic enough to keep the teenagers' attention from zooming in on Zachary St. Clair.

"Wow, Sheila, would you get a load of *that*!"

Sharon stopped, closed her eyes and sighed, convinced she could already hear the townspeople building the gallows outside her jail cell. Either that, or it's the sound of someone hammering yet another nail into my coffin, she mused, wondering if things could possibly get worse before they began to get better.

"Worse," she decided aloud, suddenly realizing that, in order to get to her office, Zachary St. Clair would first have to bend his ridiculously tall frame so that he could fit under the cut-out section in the snack bar counter. Oh, yes, she agreed with herself silently, I could lead him back outside and into the office via the projection room. But that would mean introducing him to George, and I think the poor man has had enough for one night!

Turning to face her new employer, Sharon attempted to dazzle him with another of her wide smiles, fingered an imaginary cigar beside her mouth, chirped, "Walk this way, please," in her best Groucho Marx impersonation, and then quickly bent almost in half to scurry underneath the counter.

She didn't stop until she had threaded her way through the milling employees and past the small, open door marked Private. The room she entered was slightly smaller than minuscule, containing a child-size wooden school desk and single chair, an oversize refrigerator, a green metal table laden with tools and several speakers in varying stages of disrepair, and a half dozen industrial-size boxes of soda cups, napkins and other snack bar supplies. There was no window, little light and no more room to run.

Bracing the seat of her shorts against the back of the chair, she carefully folded her arms beneath her breasts, awaiting the verbal drubbing she was sure St. Clair was about to deliver. She didn't have long to wait.

"You call this rabbit hutch an office?" he began in his smooth, educated voice.

"Actually, Mr. St. Clair, I call this office a rabbit hutch," Sharon returned almost calmly, inwardly amazing herself at her own daring. "But then, at a time like this I imagine we really shouldn't be splitting *hares*, should we?"

St. Clair looked at her steadily for a long, heart-stopping moment, during which Sharon could feel the last of her bravado cravenly folding its tent and slipping silently away, then he said, "If you could possibly bring yourself to attempt it, I have somehow retained a slim hope that this discussion can be conducted at something at least approaching an adult level."

Sharon shrugged yet again. "Sorry, Mr. St. Clair," she apologized in a sincere voice. "I'm listening. Fire away." Grimacing at what she had just said, she then shook her head and muttered softly, "Bad choice of words, Wheeler."

But St. Clair ignored her, busy with figuring out just how he could maneuver himself into a position that would allow him to close the door, locking out the intrusive sounds from the snack bar. After several unsuccessful attempts, the last of which left him standing wedged between the edge of the door and the handle to the refrigerator, he applied to Sharon for assistance.

"I'm sorry, sir," she replied, spreading her hands helplessly. "To tell you the truth, I don't remember anyone ever shutting the door before. There's never been any need."

His green eyes narrowed, St. Clair scanned the room, obviously in search of something. "No need? Then you keep the box office receipts in a safe in the projection room?"

Sharon stepped away from the chair back and belligerently thrust out her chin. "We have never found it necessary to hide the money away from our employees. Wheeler employees are honest, Mr. St. Clair. Besides, money is never kept here overnight. I use the night drop at the branch bank down the street."

That was good, that was very good, she cheered herself silently. Keep it up, Sharon, and keep your fingers crossed that he doesn't ask to see the safe anyway.

"I'd still like to see the safe, Miss Wheeler, if you don't mind," St. Clair pushed on relentlessly.

Like a dog worrying a bone, Sharon concluded, beginning to really dislike the man standing in front of her. "Don't you think you've seen enough for one evening, Mr. St. Clair?" she asked hopefully. "I'd be more than willing to meet you out here tomorrow morning—or whatever time you choose—to inspect the theater. I mean after all, what with Gertrude, and that silly woman, and all—"

"The safe, Miss Wheeler," he repeated, reaching up to loosen his tie and undo the top button of his white

silk shirt as the heat in the small office began to take
its toll.

Sharon lifted a hand to rub at the back of her slim
neck. "All right, sir," she said, capitulating. "But
never say I didn't warn you. The money is behind you,
in the lettuce keeper. Rather apt, right? Bottom shelf,
behind the chopped onions."

St. Clair turned his head slowly to stare incredulously at the white enamel door behind him, then just
as slowly looked back to stare at Sharon. "You keep
the box office receipts in the *refrigerator*?" he ground
out angrily.

Already mentally scanning the help wanted ads,
Sharon leaned back against the chair once more,
spread her arms wide and grinned. "Doesn't everybody?"

Zachary sat alone in a dark corner of the nearly deserted hotel cocktail lounge, his long, lean legs
wrapped around the bar stool as he slowly sipped his
Scotch on the rocks.

Raising his lips from the rim of the glass, he peered
desultorily into the marble-veined mirror behind the
back bar, unsurprised to see the deep lines that wea-
riness had cut into his face on either side of his mouth,
then shifted his gaze back to watch the amber liquid as
he swirled it around in the glass in front of him.

He was tired, so damnably tired. He had a solid year
of deal making, merger producing, hostile takeover
maneuvering and buy-outs behind him, the culmination of more than eight years of careful planning and
old-fashioned hard work. The St. Clair Theater Cor-

poration, begun by his father thirty years earlier with the purchase of a single indoor theater in upstate New York, had finally lived up to all expectations—thanks to the financial brilliance of Lucien St. Clair's whiz-kid son, Zachary, "the college boy."

The St. Clair Theater Corporation now owned 127 theaters in the thriving market on the Eastern seaboard, boasting 863 screens. The theaters, or houses, as they were called, were almost all automated multi-screen facilities, equipped with the most up-to-date xenon projectors, and operated under what Zachary believed to be the most modern management program in the industry.

Automation—that was the ticket to sound management. The bottom line in theater management was profit, just as it was in any other business, and projection automation, though costly to install, meant a large reduction in staff—and in the payment of salaries.

Taking another sip of his Scotch, Zachary remembered how his school-of-hard-knocks father had refused to consider the installation of automated projectors and manager-projectionists when the proposal had first been presented to him, causing their first real argument since the younger St. Clair had officially joined the company Lucien had named with him in mind.

But Lucien had at last agreed to a compromise, Zachary recalled now with a slight smile, agreeing to allow his college-educated son to automate a small regional five-theater chain the company had purchased in Delaware as a sort of test. "He wanted me to fall flat on my face," Zachary softly told the half inch of Scotch still remaining in the bottom of his glass, "but eight years and several million dollars later, I think I can safely say Dad's seen the light."

Thoughts of his self-made father, now retired and living in Florida with Zachary's shopping-mall-mad mother, brought him rudely back to reality—a reality that took the form of Wheeler's Drive-In.

"Dad would love that run-down old place," he ruminated, shaking his head. "Folksy, he'd call it." He lifted a long, pale hand and ran his fingers through one side of his coal black hair. "God, I'm tired. So tired, I'm talking out loud to myself in a public place. What's the matter with me anyway?"

Temporary burnout. That's what it is, he decided silently, looking once more into the mirror, this time inspecting his reflection with a critical eye. *I've been under a lot of pressure lately, wanting to wrap up this final deal before the end of the fiscal quarter,* he thought. *Look at my face. It's already May and I'm still so pale I look like the underbelly of a fish. I don't remember the last time I had a golf club in my hands, let alone the time for a game.*

"All work and no play make Zachary a dull boy," he paraphrased prosaically, saluting his reflection with the glass before downing the last of his drink.

"What did you say, Mister?" asked the hotel bartender, who had been making a great business out of wiping down the long mahogany bar in hopes his last customer would take the hint and hit the road. "You want another drink?"

Standing up and reaching into his pocket to deposit a large tip on the top of the bar, Zachary replied, "No, thank you anyway. I believe I'll call it a night." He began to walk slowly toward the door that led into the lobby, then stopped and turned back to ask, "You know of any good golf courses around here? I'll need to rent clubs."

"Golf courses? Of *course* I do!" the bartender quipped, unknowingly reminding Zachary of an infuriating small blonde who seemed to be equally fond of puns. "Let's see. You got your Allentown Municipal, your Twin Lakes, your Willow Brook—that's a small course—your Wedgewood. Then there's your private courses, if you know anyone who can get you on. Those would be your country clubs. You've got your Lehigh Country Club, your Brookside—"

Zachary held up his hand to stem the dizzying flow of words. "Thank you very much, I believe I get the picture. I think I might know somebody who can arrange a round at one of the private clubs," he said, remembering the local lawyer with whom he had worked concerning the purchase of the theaters. Surely the guy owed him something for not warning him about Wheeler's.

A few minutes later, lying fully dressed atop the king-size bed in his room, his arms loosely folded behind his head, Zachary could feel the tension slowly leaving his body. He'd spend the weekend playing a few rounds of golf, getting a little time in the sun to clear out the cobwebs, and then on Monday he'd call Sharon Wheeler and take her up on that offer to inspect the theater.

It was the least he could do, considering the way she had nearly begged him for the chance to make up for his poor first impression of the place. After all, he wasn't heartless. He'd give her every chance to convince him that holding on to Wheeler's Drive-In was in the best interest of his company.

And *then* he would order the place to close, tossing that obnoxious young female out on her pert little nose!

"Move it, George, please! We have two measly days in which to turn this place into a tight ship."

George Blakeman, sitting at his ease atop the cool metal lid of the ice cream freezer in the snack bar, sniffed rudely. "Tight ship? Big deal. Everybody thought the *Titanic* was a tight ship, and look what happened to it. Right? Calm down, Shari. You'd need a miracle to turn this place into the kind of theater that St. Clair wants to see, and I'm all out of loaves and fishes."

"George! That's blasphemous!" Sharon exclaimed, shocked into stopping what she was doing, which looked, as George had told her earlier, as if she was running around wildly in three directions at once—while accomplishing nothing.

Reaching up a finger to idly scratch the side of his long, bulbous nose, which had been broken more than once in his checkered lifetime, the projectionist returned calmly, "Maybe. But since the place they'll send me to can't be any hotter than that projection room in there, I don't see as how I'll even notice."

Sharon tilted her blond head to one side and narrowed her eyelids to look searchingly at her old friend. "You've been working at Wheeler's since before I was born, George. Don't you care about the place? Not even a little bit?"

The man shrugged diffidently. "I've been working here on borrowed time ever since your grandfather died, Shari, honey, and you know it. Either one of our two previous owners would have tossed me out on my ear long ago if only they'd taken the time to come see the place. Right? It just hasn't been the same, and the road keeps calling. You can't keep covering for me forever. Besides, I'm pushing seventy now and, truth to tell, when summer comes and we start opening every night instead of just weekends I don't think I'm going to be able to hack it at all anymore. Sorry."

Sharon stuck her hands on her hips and took one step toward him. "So that's it? Just like that? You're giving up? I'm disappointed in you, George, really I am. After all, you were Popsie's right-hand man. He took you in when nobody else would touch you with— oh, never mind, forget I said that. Just remember what Popsie did for you. Is this how you pay him back?"

"That was all a long time ago, honey," George argued, his thin face showing every year of his age. "There's been a lot of water under the bridge since then. Your grandfather's been gone a long time, and things just aren't the way they used to be. Besides, I paid your Popsie back for hiring me. Right? I never ran out on the job while he was alive, and you know it."

Putting her fingers to her throbbing temples, Sharon dropped her head forward slightly, guilt washing
over her at the plaintive sound in George's normally
gruff, raspy voice. "Of course you have, George. I'm
so sorry. Please forgive me. It's just—" she spread her
arms wide as if to take in the whole of the theater
"—it's just that I love this old place so much. Oh,
George, he's going to shut us down. I just know it. I
hate that Mr. Three-piece-suit St. Clair!"

George gave a weak smile. "I can hardly wait to
meet this fella, if he's everything you say he is. A real
1980s businessman, with calculator ink in his veins,
you said. But I'll bet you're only putting me on about
that pointed tail. Right?"

Sharon laughed, George's banter succeeding in
breaking her mood. "Don't forget the horns,
George," she reminded him, motioning for the man to
shift himself to one side so that she could open one of
the smaller lids on the freezer and get them each an ice
cream sandwich, George's favorite confection.

"What's this? I know what you're doing, you
sneaky child. You're trying to bribe me with ice cream.
Right? It won't change the facts, but I won't say no to
the bribe," George quipped, snatching one of the
sandwiches from her hand.

"Wretch," Sharon sniffed huffily, barely hiding her
amusement.

"Oh, yeah? Well, sticks and stones, and all that,"
George retorted happily, just to show he had forgiven
her for her earlier outburst.

"So," she said after removing the paper wrapper
and taking her first satisfying bite of ice cream, "you

think I'm beating a dead horse, don't you, trying to hang on to this place? Come on, George, sock it to me."

The projectionist waited until he had finished his ice cream, which only took him four big bites, before obliging. "The day of the drive-in theater in this part of the country is just about over, Shari, like I've told you a thousand times before. What with the multiscreen houses and the malls, there's just no need for them anymore. Like me, they've outlived their usefulness."

"But, George," Sharon interrupted, "people *like* to watch movies outdoors. It's great for families, kids—"

"In *Texas* it's good," George broke in, pointing a finger at her. "In *New Mexico* it's good. In *California* it's good. They can keep their theaters open year round. In *Pennsylvania* it's ridiculous. We can only stay open from April until September or October. In the warmer parts of the country they're even building a couple of new houses, five-screen outdoor theaters, with modern sound systems. But then, I've heard it told that it doesn't snow much in Southern California. No, the only way Wheeler's has any chance of staying alive is as a mom-and-pop operation. Right? No chain is going to cotton to a house that can only open in the summer. It's just not good business economically. You understand?"

"Now you sound like St. Clair," Sharon grumbled, wrinkling up her nose. "Before he stomped out of here last night he was mouthing words like 'green sheets' and 'bottom lines.' Do you know his corporation actually bought this place without even *looking* at it! Where has the romance of the theater gone, the thrill of ownership? To him it's nothing but a business. Doesn't anyone have any respect for the past, for the institutions that helped to make this country great?''

"Drive-in movies made this country great? They may have added a bit to the population explosion, maybe, but *made this country great*? Aren't you stretching things just a tad?''

Sharon pouted, totally frustrated. "Don't split hairs with me, George, you know what I mean. I—I just can't seem to put it into words.'' Seeing that George was about to offer her the comfort of his arms—a move that would surely reduce her to juvenile sobs— she stuck out her chin and said, "Go home, George. You're right. There's nothing we can do in this short time to change anything. Especially after Gertrude's appearance. Mr. St. Clair is just going to have to take us or leave us the way we are—and before you say it, no, you can't have odds on what he'll choose to do! I'll see you tonight about six.''

The projectionist looked at his young employer and friend carefully for a moment. Then, seeming to come to a decision, he mumbled, "Right,'' eased himself down from his perch and headed for the door. "See you at six.''

It was only after she heard the sound of George's ancient Plymouth starting up and pulling away that Sharon allowed her tense body to relax, slumping against the snack bar counter in an attitude of total defeat.

"How could I have said those things to George?" she berated herself aloud, shaking her head in self-disgust. "It isn't as if I don't know the full story, for heaven's sake!" She then closed her eyes, remembering the long-ago conversation during which her grandfather had told her the story of George Blakeman.

Back in the early 1940s, in the days before non-flammable acetate film, the projectionist's job was considered to be both the most romantic and the most dangerous in the movie theater business. Working in their underwear in the extreme heat of the high, airless booths, the projectionists, who always worked in pairs, were constantly exposed to the possibility that the film could become jammed in the projectors, causing the nitrate film to ignite. Once burning, the fire would quickly spread upward to the reel house, the metal box holding the feeding reel of film, and an explosion would result within the space of a few moments.

George's projector at the downtown theater where he worked had been involved in just such an incident. Sharon could almost hear Popsie's voice as he recounted the drama of the incident. "It all happened so quickly, Poppet. One minute George and his assistant were laughing about one of the girls in the snack bar who had a crush on George, and the next moment the film in George's projector jammed, concentrating all the white-hot light from the carbon lamp on a single frame of film. George tried to shut down the lamp house but it was already too late. Bang, the fire shot right up into the film house. Then all hell broke loose."

Sharon shivered as she pictured the scene. There were no windows in such a projection room, only four holes cut into the walls abutting the theater proper, two to let the film be shown, and two for the projectionists to look through. As the fire grew, the special lead safety fuse holding the chain that in turn held the steel plates that sat just above each of the four small openings melted in the heat, and the plates dropped into position, closing the holes with loud bangs like cell doors slamming. The room was submerged in total darkness.

Both projectionists knew they now had only a few moments to get out of the booth before the burning film inside the metal reel house caused it to explode. They had to grope for the door to the hallway in the dark, get through it as quickly as possible and then try to contain the explosion by shutting the door behind them.

George made it out.

His friend didn't. The man's burns had put him in the hospital for more than a year, and George held himself responsible.

"George was one of the best in the business," Sharon remembered Popsie telling her as she, her ten-year-old skinny, tanned bare legs kicking back and forth as she perched on the workbench in the drive-in projection booth, hung on her grandfather's every word. "But he was never the same after that day, poor fella. He drinks sometimes, you understand, just to stop the memories, but mostly he just goes off on his own, to sulk. He's still one hell of a projectionist. He'll never let you down, Poppet, I can guarantee it."

"And he never did, Popsie," Sharon murmured aloud now, slowly wiping away a tear. "But I think I'm finally asking too much of the poor old dear. It's clear that George just doesn't have it in him to fight St. Clair. Besides, even if the theater could by some miracle get a second life, St. Clair is bound to want to replace George's faithful Gloria and Veronica with two of those new xenon projectors. The poor guy just couldn't take that, it would break his heart. I couldn't ask it of him. It's over. It's all over."

Closing her eyes against the realization that there was nothing she could do to halt the closing of Wheeler's, Sharon picked up the damp towel she had been using to bring a high sheen to the chrome butter dispenser, tossed it carelessly onto one slim shoulder and walked out of the snack bar into the bright Saturday morning sunlight.

Chapter Three

It had been a full house Saturday night, thanks to pleasant weather and the popularity of *Spy in the Eye* with the largely teenage crowd, and Sharon was feeling a bit more confident about the theater, the future and life in general that Sunday morning on her drive to the Lehigh Country Club and her weekly game with her friend Hugh Kingsley, who considered her his permanent guest partner on the golf course.

Tonight would mark the final showing of the adventure film, but Sharon wasn't too worried about the success of next weekend's offering, a parental-guidance-suggested adventure film and, by some stroke of luck she didn't care to look into too deeply, a first-run Disney movie as their feature presentation. Unless the weather refused to cooperate, Wheeler's should realize another very profitable weekend run.

Yes, Sharon was happy, and she was looking forward to the golf match ahead of her.

She arrived at the country club just after ten, once the worst of the crush of golfers had teed off and, after donning her golf shoes in the parking lot because she loved the sound the metal spikes made while crunching across the graveled lot, made her way to the pro shop to meet Hugh.

Her clubs and bag, both gifts from her grandfather, were already securely strapped to the back of one of the white motorized golf carts, for Hugh had long ago convinced her of the foolishness of refusing his offer to store her clubs in the locker room at his expense. After all, he had reasoned, it was cheaper for him to do that than to pay off the seven million dollars in bets he owed her in their five-year-old-and-still-running gin rummy competition.

Rounding the corner of the white-painted brick pro shop at a brisk pace, Sharon smiled and waved gaily as she saw Hugh Kingsley turn away from the two men he was speaking with and motion her to join him under the wooden canopy. Her smile faded, however, when she realized just who was standing in the shadows beside Hugh on the bricked patio.

"Zachary St. Clair," she fairly hissed, nearly tripping over her own feet as she stumbled to a halt, a flush of confusion mixed with anger flooding into her cheeks. "Maybe somebody's put a curse on me, and I just don't know it yet. Please, please *don't* let him be playing along with Hugh and me. *Please!*"

* * *

Zachary and his lawyer companion, Fred Staples, had spent an enjoyable afternoon on the course Saturday, followed by a quick dip in the club pool and a leisurely dinner in the main dining room. So congenial was their day that Fred, a bachelor himself, had asked Zachary to join him for a repeat of their activities again today. The young lawyer didn't have a regular foursome on Sundays, so he was free to make the invitation, and he had asked the golf pro to arrange a foursome for him.

What Zachary didn't know, information that most probably would have had him hastily declining Fred's generous offer, was that the pro had managed to pair them up with Hugh Kingsley, a local hotel owner, and his female partner.

A woman golfer, Zachary was thinking as the blond-haired woman approached. *Just what I need. I can only hope she and this Kingsley fellow are engaged or something, or I could end up spending the day trying to fend off her obvious advances as she asks me to help her with her swing.*

If Zachary had voiced this thought aloud his companions would have thought him egotistical in the extreme, but then neither Hugh nor Fred had witnessed the many close calls Zachary's extreme good looks and favorable fortune had caused on the links, in dark hallways and on secluded beaches between Florida and Maine.

Now, looking once more at the woman, who had for some reason or another stopped some distance away from the small group, Zachary slowly reassessed his first reaction.

She presented quite an attractive picture, dressed as she was in a thin, sleeveless, scoop-necked cotton blouse that had a row of tiny buttons running neck to waist between attractively rounded breasts and a knee-length grass-green culotte that cinched tightly at her small waist and revealed straight, tanned legs that ended in low green socks and white golf shoes. Her shoulder-length honey-blond hair, he noticed, was held away from her face by a white terry visor that shadowed her features, allowing the sun to highlight only her finely sculpted chin line and full, pouting mouth.

Strange, Zachary thought, wrinkling his brow slightly, *but that mouth almost looks familiar. But that's impossible, isn't it?* "Oh, no!" he whispered hoarsely after a moment, leaning forward slightly to stare at the woman, who had at last moved to join them. "It couldn't be!"

"Zachary," Hugh was saying congenially, "I'd like you to meet my golfing partner, good friend and ruthless opponent, Sharon Wheeler. Sharon, please allow me—"

"It is!" Zachary mumbled almost under his breath, Hugh's voice fading into the background as Sharon gingerly held out her hand. Taking it automatically, Zachary was struck, as he had been on Friday evening, by the smallness, the seeming fragility of Sharon Wheeler's hand.

"Mr. St. Clair and I have already met, Hugh. It would seem that he's my new boss," Zachary heard her say, and he mentally shook himself into speech.

"Too true, Miss Wheeler," he then heard himself reply. "But if you'll allow me to use a movie title to express my feelings about our business relationship, please, *Never on Sunday*. It's entirely too nice today to be talking shop, don't you think?"

I think I'd like to do to you what the hero of Spy in the Eye *did to Dr. Death—but then there's never a handy pit of molten lava around when a girl needs one,* Sharon thought privately, deciding that the only thing worse than a frowning, obnoxious St. Clair was a smiling, obnoxious St. Clair.

Aloud, however, with her hand still tingling from its encounter with his, she only said, "I bow to the wisdom of my employer." Then, turning to his companion, she immediately launched into a long discussion with Fred about the court case he had won that week, a victory that had earned him quite a bit of good local press.

Ten minutes later the foursome, having hit their tee shots down the first fairway, were barreling after their balls in two motorized carts—and Sharon Wheeler had not so much as looked in Zachary's direction.

By the time the foursome got to the third hole, Zachary had become grudgingly appreciative of Sharon's form on the tee, her controlled swing with a chipping wedge and her accuracy with a putter. She was a good golfer, better than Hugh, her partner.

By the time they had completed the sixth hole, his appreciation had become less that of a competitor and more that of a man for a woman.

After all, he would have to be blind not to notice the fine line of Sharon's slim body as she leaned over to mark her ball on the putting green.

He would have to be an eunuch not to notice the way the soft white material of her blouse tautened across her firm, high breasts as she held the driver above her head and watched the progress of her ball after completing her follow-through off the tee.

And he would have to be deaf not to enjoy her sharp, witty banter with the other two men who made up the foursome; two men whose easy relationship with Sharon—even whose very presence on the golf course—Zachary was rapidly beginning to resent with a passion that shocked him to his core.

Perhaps this was why, after teeing off on the seventh hole, Zachary found it hard to maintain a solemn expression when Hugh suggested that, since both their balls had hit to the right side of the fairway, Sharon and Zachary share a golf cart as they all rode to their second shots.

"But my clubs are on your cart, Hugh," Sharon protested as she bent down to retrieve her tee and secure it between the laces of one of her golf shoes.

"No problem, Sharon," Hugh said, reaching into her bag and drawing out the three iron. "Here, take this with you. Unless you think it's going to take you two shots to reach the green. I'll be waiting there with your putter."

"Sure you will, Hugh," Sharon shot back, snatching the club from his hand. "Would that be before or after you dig your own ball out of the sand trap?"

"Ouch!" the hotel owner said, wincing comically at the verbal slap. "I forgot you were with me that day." Turning to Zachary, he explained, "Sharon has just been so kind as to bring up something I'd rather forget. A few weeks ago I was buried so deep in that trap off to the left of the green that by the time I got done swiping at the blasted ball I thought I could see glimpses of Hong Kong."

"Then that wasn't a fortune cookie you had stuck in your mouth when you finally climbed up onto the green?" Sharon asked, smiling at her partner. "All right, Mr. St. Clair," she then said, sighing a little, "I'm ready. It's a little tricky getting down to the fairway from this hill. Do you want me to drive?"

"I think I can handle it, *Miss* Wheeler," Zachary told her. Sharon's words had reminded him of his accident three years earlier. He should have known better than to let his guard down, no matter how easy Sharon Wheeler was on the eyes. When it came to hitting his sore spots, she seemed to have some inner radar that told her just where to probe. "If you'll notice," he told her from between clenched teeth as he walked to the driver's side of the cart, "after playing the course without incident yesterday I've been allowed to navigate without training wheels today."

Sharon laughed aloud at his joke, but Zachary was sure she had done it only for Fred's and Hugh's benefit. He was close enough to see that her smile hadn't quite reached her eyes.

Her beautiful, cornflower-blue eyes.

Sharon turned straight ahead immediately after waving the two men to her left on their way, but the slight breeze that lifted her hair from her nape sent a faint hint of perfume wafting in Zachary's direction.

Her flowery scent that, against his will, teased and tantalized him.

"There's another path to this side of the tee, Mr. St. Clair," she informed him woodenly. "Once you pull forward slightly you'll be able to see it."

"Thank you, *Sharon*," he answered smoothly, stepping sharply on the accelerator and causing the cart to start off with a small lurching movement.

The woman was beginning to drive him out of his mind! The sooner he got this hole over with the better, he reasoned, then wondered why he was disappointed to see that no ball-trapping woods lay to the right of the seventh hole. "You don't mind if I call you Sharon, at least for the rest of the day, do you? I certainly don't mind if you call me Zachary. After all, it seems silly to be so formal when we're all out here trying to enjoy ourselves."

"Meaning you're not really enjoying yourself, *Zachary*?" she asked him, still keeping her gaze glued to the macadam cart path in front of them. "I seem to recall that you have a somewhat limited sense of humor. Perhaps you're disappointed that we aren't playing for money?"

"Meaning?" Zachary asked, his green eyes narrowed.

"Meaning, *Zachary*, that you only seem to be interested in ventures that can be measured by a balance sheet—a bottom line."

"I said I didn't wish to discuss business today," Zachary shot back tersely, drawing alongside Sharon's ball and stopping the cart. "There's your ball. You honestly believe you'll reach the green from here? But, as you play this course a lot, I guess you know what you're doing."

"Sure, that figures," she said, seemingly addressing the club in her hand. "I strike a nerve and he immediately changes the subject—or runs away, like he did Friday night."

Zachary grabbed Sharon's arm just above the elbow, interrupting her descent from the cart, her one foot already on the grass as she swiveled her head sharply to look at him. "On the contrary. I was just trying to be polite after you said something singularly ridiculous, comparing my work to a game of golf."

"I did not! I admit that it might have sounded that way, but I merely said that—"

"The St. Clair Theater Corporation isn't just a small hobby of mine, Miss Wheeler. Or a game to be enjoyed," he persevered, cutting her off. "I have stockholders to answer to, and sharks in the water ready to try to take over if the business should show signs of stumbling in any way. Please forgive me if I fail to find any *humor* in that."

Looking pointedly at his hand, which was still wrapped around her arm, then up into his eyes, Sharon said passionately, "Well, all right, but that's no excuse for calling my theater a disaster zone and then stomping off like some spoiled child without even giving me a chance to show you the place. There's been no money put into improvements in nearly ten years. Of course there are problems, but they're only physical. You refused to see any of the charm of the place."

"Charm?" Zachary sneered. "Oh, yes, I remember now. You must be talking about the bucolic scene I witnessed, with Mrs. Harrison's cows grazing so elegantly between the rows of parked cars. How could I not have been struck with the beauty, the serenity of the scene?"

"Don't be sarcastic," Sharon ordered, finally succeeding in pulling her arm free.

"No, no. Please, Miss Wheeler, allow me to defend myself. You're accusing me of being humorless, and a man devoid of an appreciation of—what was it—oh, yes, *the charm of the place*! Is that what you call keeping the box office receipts in a lettuce bowl? Because if it is, I must tell you that I'd find the practice extremely charming—if my mother did it! For a business to do it is just plain stupid!"

"Hey! Are you going to hit, Shari, or just sit there hoping a stiff wind comes along and blows the ball onto the green?"

"She's almost ready, Fred," Zachary called back across the fairway to the two men waiting in the other cart. "She was worried about the three iron not being enough club for the shot."

"Liar," Sharon muttered, rounding the cart to approach the ball. "Very glib, but still a liar. And, oh, so careful to put the blame on somebody else."

"Just hit the ball, Miss Wheeler," Zachary told her. "Pretend you see my face painted on it and you may just overshoot the green."

Her feet spread about a foot apart, her hands already positioned in an interlocking grip, Sharon raised her head to look at her companion, her big blue eyes sparkling with anticipation. "With pleasure, *Mr.* St. Clair!"

Okay, Wheeler, Sharon told herself as she climbed back into the cart alongside Hugh and allowed herself to be driven to the eighth tee. *So you had a par and Mr. High-and-Mighty St. Clair took a bogie. Do you feel better now? No, you don't,* she answered her own mental question, shaking her head. *I believe that's what they call winning the battle only to lose the war.*

She might have shown him up back there, putting that chip shot within two feet of the cup, but she sure as heck lost the war of words out there on the fairway—kissing goodbye any lingering chance to keep Wheeler's open. What a way to get the boss on your side—by insulting him!

Turning to look at Hugh, she said aloud, "Hugh, have you got any jobs open at that hotel of yours for an unemployed theater manager? I think I just talked myself out of a job back there with St. Clair."

"You, Shari?" Hugh asked, a puzzled expression on his face. "I don't believe it."

"Believe it, Hugh. Every time I come within ten feet of that man I either insult him or—come to think of it, at least I've been consistent. I just seem to insult him. Anyway, the man doesn't like me."

"Don't be ridiculous. Everybody likes you, Shari, even my mother," Hugh assured her, smiling. *"Especially* my mother. She keeps after me to get married and settle down. You, my dear, are her number-one candidate. I keep telling her that I can't marry someone who beats me so mercilessly in golf, at cards, even on the tennis court; but she won't listen. I think she's hoping you'll keep me humble. Sorry, but it's the only job I've got open at the moment. Interested?"

Sharon reached across the small space separating them in the cart and kissed her friend on the cheek. "Thanks, Hugh, but I think I'll pass—you nut! Doesn't your mother understand that we're just good friends?"

"That's us, Shari," the handsome young hotel owner returned, smiling. "Just good friends. Now come here, friend, and give me a real kiss. I just took a double bogey and I need some cheering up. Besides, you're much more fun in a golf cart than old Fred."

"Nut!" Sharon scolded happily, then leaned sideways to allow herself to be kissed.

Zachary had his worst round of golf in his recent memory, but he refused to acknowledge that his troubles had all begun on the seventh hole, then doubled after he saw Sharon and Hugh doing their lovers' routine on the way to the eighth tee.

What did he care what Sharon Wheeler and Hugh Kingsley did, even if it was mighty poor golf etiquette? They should have just steered the cart off into the bushes and rejoined him and Fred on the back nine after they'd gotten all that juvenile need for a public display of passion out of their systems, because he sure didn't need to be treated to another such scene. You'd think they'd been parted for years, not just for the length of one hole, the way they had fallen all over each other in the cart.

Hugh Kingsley could just count himself lucky that he'd kept his paws off Sharon for the remainder of the round!

Get a hold on yourself, boy! Zachary ordered, giving himself a mental kick at the violence of his thoughts as he nursed his third ice-cold diet soda in the clubhouse, waiting for the rest of the foursome to join him after their showers. *It's none of my business if, at this very moment, Hugh is dragging my manager across the parking lot by her hair, taking her back to his blasted hotel for a night of sin and decadence. I couldn't care less, dammit.* Zachary was still too tense, still overreacting to things that normally wouldn't bother him. *Just be careful,* he warned himself. He still had the rest of this day and the next morning to get through before he could get back to New York and away from that ridiculous woman.

That woman.

Sharon Wheeler. How that small blonde had gotten under his skin! He couldn't understand it.

Okay, so she has a beautiful face and body, he conceded. So did every female he dated, and he had dated quite a few.

Yes, she played one tremendous game of golf. So did Jan Stephenson, another blonde, yet he had never felt any urge to drag the beautiful, calendar-posing golf professional off into the bushes and kiss *her* until she was senseless.

So what was it about Sharon that so attracted him to her, infuriated him while not repelling him in the slightest?

Funny, he thought, shaking his head, *but she reminds me a bit of my father.* How he loved the theaters, much more than he ever loved the business. Zachary remembered the many times he and his father had gone head to head, as the younger man tried to pull the older—kicking and screaming all the way—into the modern world of theater ownership.

Zachary loved the arguments, the mind games, the confrontations he had faced, first with his father, and then with the men with whom he sought to do business—men who initially refused to take him seriously, who found it hard to believe that "daddy's little boy" actually knew the difference between a projection booth and a tollbooth, let alone anything they themselves didn't know.

But in the past few years the sheer size and power of the St. Clair Theater Corporation had done most of his fighting for him, and the thrill of the chase had somehow disappeared. Today, and for at least three years, he had been going through the motions, but feeling none of the satisfaction of ownership. He was ready for a challenge, primed for a good old-fashioned toe-to-toe fight. He had been accumulating "screens," not purchasing "theaters."

He took a quick drink from his glass, suddenly feeling guilty.

Maybe that's why she's gotten to me—the way she argues with me, stands up straight and all but dares me to prove that I care about something more than just the black ink in a ledger book. "That's ridiculous," he mumbled aloud then, putting down his halfful glass with a small thump as he realized that he was beginning to feel slightly queasy from all that carbonation. "What do I care about Sharon Wheeler's opinion of me?"

It's good I don't care, he told himself, chuckling a bit under his breath, *because I can just bet my bottom dollar I'm not number one on her Christmas list this year.*

Absently utilizing the bottom of his glass to make a design of round wet circles on the shiny wood tabletop, Zachary tried very hard to understand just why Sharon's dislike of him intrigued him so much.

Looking up from his small decorating project long enough to see a well-built redhead looking across the room at him speculatively, he found the answer to his question. Sharon Wheeler was an exception—a woman who didn't throw herself at him, or use her beauty to manipulate him, or try to charm him into seeing things her way.

No, she didn't use any of the female tactics he had been used to facing ever since he'd reached his middle teens and his physical appearance and his father's income had both risen to "handsome" heights. And, Zachary acknowledged, it wasn't as if she hadn't the ammunition for such an assault either, because she was one very beautiful lady.

Ah, but she doesn't like you, Zachary St. Clair, he pointed out to himself, *she doesn't like you one little bit.*

He was back to square one, understanding more of the questions, perhaps, but still not coming up with any workable answers.

"So," Hugh Kingsley said heartily, interrupting Zachary's private thoughts by coming up to the table and seating himself in one of the large captain's chairs, "I guess you'll be heading back to New York tomorrow, you lucky devil. What I wouldn't give for a few days in the Big Apple."

His teeth are too white, Zachary thought idly as he returned Hugh's smile. *His teeth are too white and his face is too tan. He's probably never worked a full day in his life.* "Actually, Hugh," he heard himself saying, "this weekend has proved to be too short. What I really need is a good, long vacation, and Allentown is as good a place as any. I can take my time inspecting my latest acquisitions firsthand instead of sending in my usual team and relax a bit at the same time."

"Really," Hugh answered, the flat tone of his voice doing wonders for Zachary's mood.

"Yes," he went on as he rose to his feet to hold out a chair for Sharon, who, along with Fred Staples, was just joining them, "I think the personal touch is just what my new theaters need."

Hugh Kingsley's very white teeth disappeared behind his tightly shut lips for a moment before he smiled once more and said, rather hollowly, "The personal touch. How nice."

"Yes," Zachary agreed, motioning to the waiter, "yes, indeed. Suddenly I find myself ravenously hungry. Anyone else? My treat."

Chapter Four

The moment Sharon pulled her car onto the theater grounds early Sunday evening she knew something was wrong. Sam, who was usually at his post at the ticket booth, setting up the cash box and hanging up a new reel of tickets over the nail hammered into the wall, was nowhere in sight. Neither was Denny, Sam's assistant.

"They're probably up at the snack bar getting themselves some sodas," she assured herself aloud, trying hard to quell the nervous fluttering that had suddenly invaded her midsection.

She guided her car past the first four rows of speakers, then turned into the fifth row, heading for the small parking area behind the snack bar that couldn't be used for patrons because the roof of the building interfered with the view of the screen.

George's Plymouth was already there and she breathed a quick sigh of relief until she realized that the old car was sitting at an awkward angle, looking as if it had not been parked, but abandoned.

"Dammit, George!" she exclaimed, pounding one small fist against the steering wheel. "Not now! Of all the times in the world, why did you have to pick *now*?"

She was out of her compact car almost before the engine died, running for the snack bar. After scuttling under the cutout in the Formica bar, she skidded around the center island holding the steamer table and soda dispensers, to arrive, breathless, at the doorway to the projection booth.

"Where is he?"

Sam, his balding head bent close to check Veronica's lamp house, answered without turning around. "He's in your office. Denny's pouring some coffee down him now. He'll be fine by show time. Denny and I have the house trailer ready on Gloria and the first reel's all threaded up here on Veronica, so you've got plenty of time."

"Thanks, Sam," Sharon said fervently, knowing that Denny and Sam were doing all they could to help cover for George. "Now if only you guys could find a way to take tickets *and* run the projectors, we'd be home free."

"That's the trick, isn't it, Shari? We know how to thread them up, Denny and me, but neither of us can run them worth a darn. Just get George another gallon of coffee, and we'll make it yet."

"Either that, or I'll wave the open can of jalapeño peppers under his nose," Sharon called back over her shoulder as she crossed the snack bar on her way to the office.

Denny, a half-empty cup in one hand and a steaming glass pot of coffee in the other, stepped back from the projectionist, who sat slumped over the small desk, as Sharon edged her way sideways into the small room. "We found him hanging over Gloria in the booth, mumbling something about the good old days. He's really tied one on, Shari. Poor guy."

"That you, Shari?" George croaked, lifting his head from its resting place on his crossed arms. "I'll be fine in a minute, honest I will. I was just drinking a few toasts to Gloria and Veronica, sort of a goodbye party, you know. I guess things got a little out of hand. Right?"

Sharon's heart was nearly breaking to see her old friend and mentor in such a sorry state. He usually just takes himself off to sit in a dark theater all day, Sharon thought, deciding that he must be very upset. She closed her eyes in mingled sorrow and frustration, wondering which emotion, pity or anger, would win the battle raging inside her.

"Oh, George, you poor darling! *He* did this to you, didn't he?"

Even as she was cradling the now sobbing George against her slim shoulder she didn't realize that both emotions had found an outlet; pity directed at George, her old friend, and anger directed at Zachary St. Clair, the bogeyman who was about to take away George's last reason for living....

George gave it his best shot, but although his mind seemed steady enough, his legs refused to cooperate, and in the end Sam and Denny had to man the projectors, with George propped up in one cool, dark corner of the booth, directing their movements.

Sharon took over duty in the ticket booth, hoping against hope that the Sunday night crowd would not descend on the theater all at once, giving her time to pass each car through the gate without allowing the line to back up onto the highway.

She was doing fine for a while, counting noses inside each car and then dispensing tickets and lollipops accordingly, greeting many of Wheeler's regulars, who always made it a point to arrive early in order to have plenty of time for either the playground or stock-up visits to the snack bar.

It was only as dusk began to fall that the line of cars suddenly became too much for one person to handle and Sharon began to wish for another pair of hands to help her.

"Where's the redheaded kid with the mouthful of bubble gum? He should be here to help you."

Sharon, in the midst of making change from a twenty dollar bill, answered the question without turning around. "Sean's studying for finals. I gave him the night off to— *What are you doing here?*"

"And a good evening to you, too, Miss Wheeler," Zachary said, putting one sneaker-clad foot onto the cement floor of the small, double-doored ticket booth, then following it with the rest of his tall, lean body. "I was beginning to get bored back at the hotel and thought I'd come out here to Wheeler's and look around a bit—hoping against hope that Gertrude won't get the itch to travel again so soon, of course. Need some help?''

Just what I don't need! Sharon thought anxiously, remembering George back in the projection booth. After hurrying through one more transaction, she took the time to look anxiously at her employer and adversary, frantically trying to figure out some way to convince him she didn't need his help.

He's beginning to get a tan, she found herself thinking rather irrationally. *It looks good with his green eyes. Maybe it's the green shirt and white slacks that set off the tan so well. His hair looks nice, too, so dark, and more casual with that small bit in the front falling down over his forehead like that, and the hair at his neck is still a bit damp and curling, like he just stepped out of the shower.*

I think I can actually smell the cleanness of him. The hair on his forearms is already bleached almost blond from the sun, and his hands look almost beautiful. He doesn't look anything like a stuffed shirt tonight; he looks more like he did this afternoon on the golf course, not that I really noticed, *with him being so totally obnoxious and all. Now he's smiling at me, actually acting human. I wonder why he's—*

''Hey, lady, get a move on! I've been holding out my hand so long with this money I'm gettin' a cramp already. What's the matter with you? Don't tell me you're sold out.''

''Wha—what?'' Sharon asked absently, still staring at Zachary's cheek-creasing smile and wondering how she could have been so blind to his masculine attractions.

"The gentleman would like to pay for his tickets, Sharon," Zachary supplied helpfully, putting out a hand to gently move her unprotesting body out of the way while he ripped four tickets off the large roll and swiftly completed the transaction, even remembering to place two lollipops in the outstretched little hands hanging over the back seat.

"Thank you, Mr.—er—thanks, Zachary," Sharon stumbled at last, shaking her head in the hope that the action would serve to bring her back to her senses before she made an utter fool of herself. "You did that very well."

"Thank *you*, Sharon," she heard him reply as he motioned through the front window of the booth for the second car in line to pull to the other side of the booth. "I used to spend my summers helping my father in our indoor theaters in New York. Of course I can't remember ever thinking that a can of insect repellent would come in handy. The mosquitoes always this bad? Three, madam? Here you go. Please be sure to visit our snack bar, and I hope you enjoy the show."

"Your next customer's in a van. Tell him to park at one of the yellow speaker poles—they're higher," Sharon heard herself saying as she snapped back to attention and began waiting on people driving up to her side of the booth. He's being nice, she told herself in disbelief. He's being *extremely* nice. *Why?*

The phone in the booth rang then, and Sharon jumped to answer it, listening for a minute while she waited on another customer, then telling the caller the first show would start when it got dark, in about half an hour.

"Why don't you get an answering machine?" Zachary asked her after she had hung up. "We have them in all our theaters. It would save you a lot of time."

Sharon shook her head. "We do use a machine during the day, but it wouldn't work for the evenings. People are always calling to ask for directions to the theater and things like that."

Zachary was silent for a moment, as if he were considering her answer. "I wish I had thought of that," he said at last, smiling at her. "I drove around forever on Friday looking for this place. It never occurred to me to call for directions. I figured I'd just get one of those damned machines."

"You mean like the kind you just got done saying we should have?" Sharon quipped. "You forget, Zachary. Wheeler's believes in the personal, human touch."

"Don't forget the homey touch, little one," he said easily, reaching up to pull four more tickets off the roll. "Your ticket dispensing 'machine,' in fact, this entire booth, could only be called 'rustic.'"

Instantly Sharon bristled. "It serves its purpose," she returned coldly, turning her back to him. So much for thinking the man was softening a bit, she rued silently, already wondering how she was going to get rid of him once this rush was over.

"My daughter wants to hand you the money for our tickets," she heard a man saying, and she turned in time to see Zachary holding out his hand to the opened

car window. "Give the nice man the money, Jennifer."

"No!" Jennifer declared, her long pigtails slapping about her shoulders as she shook her head.

"Jennifer!" her father yelled from behind the
steering wheel, which was on the other side of the car,
away from the ticket booth. "Give the nice man the
money!"

"No! Don't want to," Jennifer answered, clutching the ten dollar bill tightly to her pajama-clad chest.

Okay, Mr. I-can-do-anything St. Clair, Sharon
challenged silently, trying hard to hide her amusement. Let's see you try to charm your way out of this
one.

"I'll trade you a lollipop for the money, sweet-
heart," Zachary bargained in an encouraging voice.

"Don't like lollipops," Jennifer pouted.

"If you give me the money, I'll give you these pretty
tickets," Zachary promised, holding out the bribe en-
ticingly.

"Tickets are dumb," little Jennifer told him, eyeing him carefully.

"*Jennifer Marie Simpson*, you listen to me!" Jennifer's father, clearly angry now, ordered, trying
without success to catch hold of his daughter from the
front seat.

"I'll give you a kiss if you give me the money,"
Zachary promised softly, leaning down to rest his elbows on the car door. Sharon stood openmouthed,
watching Zachary St. Clair winking at a four-year-old
child.

"Right here?" Jennifer asked, pointing to one chubby cheek.

"Right there."

"And Stephanie, too?" the child bargained, holding up a battered, well-loved doll.

Something happened to Sharon in the few moments it took for Zachary to bend down and bestow his favors on Stephanie and Jennifer, something she didn't really desire to investigate too closely. But when he straightened once more and turned to her, a smile of delighted satisfaction lighting his newly tanned face, she knew she didn't have to examine her reaction.

Against all her better judgment, weighed up along with her innate distrust of big businessmen in general, Sharon knew she was beginning to like Zachary St. Clair.

Even worse, she was beginning to look at him the way a woman looks at a man.

Suddenly, in the barely waning heat of early evening, Sharon shivered.

The last car straggled through the gates about fifteen minutes after the movie had already begun and Sharon finally closed the lid on the cash box and reached up to remove the roll of tickets from the nail. Zachary, who had also reached up for the tickets, purposely allowed their hands to meet, watching for Sharon's reaction to their slight physical collision.

He wasn't disappointed. Sharon's hand sprang away from the contact with lightning quickness and her cheeks immediately flushed an extremely becoming pale pink beneath her golden tan. He rather liked the expression of maidenly confusion that crept into her lovely, clear blue eyes before she lowered her lids to hide her reaction.

Slowly, as Sharon stood quite still in front of the low shelf under the front window of the booth, Zachary took the cash box she was holding and returned it to its spot on the shelf. Just as slowly, he took her by the shoulders and turned her to face him in the nearly total darkness inside the small wooden shed.

"Just how close are you and Hugh Kingsley?" he asked quietly, putting one finger under her chin so that he could look into her eyes while she answered.

"Hugh?" she questioned, blinking, her T-shirt-covered breasts rising and falling rapidly in innocent enticement as she seemed to be having trouble gaining her breath. "We—we're friends. Just good friends."

"You have any other 'good friends?' Any—boy-friends?"

"Just—just George, the projectionist. He's almost seventy, though. And Sam. And Denny. They work here."

"And how old are they—Sam and Denny?" Zachary prodded, allowing his hands to slowly slide off Sharon's shoulders and down her bare arms to her elbows, the action meant to ease her body closer against him.

"I—I don't know. They're just—older. Married. Denny even met his wife here, fifteen years ago. Why?"

Zachary could feel an actual knot painfully tightening his insides as he watched Sharon wet her lips with the tip of her tongue, showing him her nervousness. "Because I don't like poaching on another man's territory, Sharon. Because I don't want to lose my head over you if you're involved with some other man. Because," he ended seriously, realizing he too was a bit breathless, "I'm going to kiss you, Sharon Wheeler. Right now."

Her lips were warm, as if kissed by the sun, and the taste of her mouth was sweet, like silken honey licked straight from the honeycomb. The well-conditioned muscles of her slim lower back served to fashion an enticing little hollow against her spine, and he could feel his fingers tingling as they lightly stroked the area, feeling her, learning her, drawing her softness against his own firm muscles.

He could again smell the flowery scent he had noticed earlier that day, and he lifted his mouth away from hers to bury his face in her unbound hair, savoring its texture. "Honey," he whispered against her ear. "Your scent, your skin, your hair, your mouth—you're as sweet, as delicious, as honey. I can't believe it."

Then his lips trailed a row of kisses back across her cheek to find her mouth once more and he felt his control begin to slip as her arms, which had remained tight to her sides, slowly reached up behind him to clasp him firmly around the neck, as if actively seeking his kiss.

"Hey, in there! Are we too late to see the show? Hey! What are you two doing in there? Making out? Fan-*tastic*! This is better than the movie!"

Zachary's mind did a quick battle with his body as his common sense told him that Sharon, now leaning weakly against him, was in no condition to handle the car full of teenage boys now parked beside the booth, its engine rumbling loudly as the driver continuously revved the motor.

Reluctantly shifting Sharon's unresisting form so that she could lean against the low shelf, he quickly opened the cash box and took care of the customers, then coughed as the car pulled away, leaving a large blue cloud of dirty exhaust fumes in its wake.

When he turned around once more, Sharon was gone.

Oh, my Lord, I can't believe I did that! I can't believe I actually did that! I let Zachary St. Clair kiss me. Worse—I kissed him back! Sharon silently beat herself over the head with self-disgust as she slammed her sneakered feet into the loose gravel on her way back across the theater lot to the snack bar.

"No, Mr. St. Clair," she gibed aloud in a singsong voice, "I don't have any boyfriends, Mr. St. Clair; George is seventy years old, Mr. St. Clair; Denny met his wife here, Mr. St. Clair; *three bags full, Mr. St. Clair!* Oh, God, what an idiot you are, Sharon Wheeler! What a complete and total idiot!"

Reaching the front end of the building, the half housing the projection booth, Sharon slammed through the entrance to see Sam and Denny working together to make a reel change, while George, yet another cup of black coffee in his hands, supervised from his place in the corner.

"That damned door is supposed to be locked at all times, and you know it," she shot out testily, never slowing her pace as she walked behind the two large floor-mounted projectors and headed for the snack bar. "And for God's sake don't goof up in here. The boss is on the grounds."

"St. Clair? Here?" George said, quickly gulping down some more of the hot coffee. "What do we do now, Shari?"

Halting for a moment in the doorway, Sharon put her hands on her hips and looked slowly around the room, seeing the reel holding the film for the house trailer and previews as well as the first reel of the film now in progress lying on their sides on the workbench, still not rewound and put back in their cases. "We get it in gear—fast. *That's* what we do. I'll be right back."

The first person Sharon saw when she entered the snack bar was Sheila, the teenager who had been working at Wheeler's for the past two years. Knowing she could count on the girl to take control of the intermission crowd that would begin descending on the snack bar in less than an hour, she quietly called her aside and delivered several quick, broad orders.

"It's Sunday night and the crowd won't be overwhelming," she told the girl, putting her arm around her and walking with her to a corner of the snack bar. "We can't save them until Friday, so push the hot dogs and turkey barbecue. If it looks like they aren't moving, offer a free soda with each sandwich, okay?"

"Yeah, sure Sharon, but—"

Sharon didn't let the girl finish. "The popcorn supply looks good, but I think you ought to get Marianne to restock the candy shelves. In about fifteen minutes have Gail start pouring out sodas and lining them up on top of the ice cream freezer. The girls all have got to take their share of the load. Push them if you have to. You're in charge, Sheila, and I'm counting on you."

"But where are you going to be?" Sheila asked as Sharon began to walk away. "You're always here for intermission."

"I'm going to help in the projection booth. George isn't feeling well and Denny has to help patrol the grounds as ramp boy because Sean has the night off. Don't call me if it isn't an emergency, okay?"

Sheila tilted her head to one side, looking puzzled. "I didn't know you could work the projectors, Shari. You never have before."

Sharon allowed herself a small smile. "I'm still a card-carrying projectionist, even if I haven't run Gloria or Veronica for a long time. But I may be a little rusty, so just hope the film doesn't break in the middle of one of the chase scenes."

Then, just as Sheila was about to inform the rest of the crew that she was in charge for the evening, Sharon added, almost as an afterthought, "Oh, yes. Sheila—I'm not to be disturbed, understand? I mean, if someone were to come in here asking for me, just tell him, er, I mean, just tell them that..." Her voice trailed off. She saw the teenager's eyes widen as Sheila's attention was taken by someone standing on the other side of the Formica counter.

"You forgot the box office receipts and the tickets," she heard Zachary say in his deep, rather husky voice.

You may run, Wheeler, she told herself, trying not to wince, but you can't hide. Taking a long, steadying breath, Sharon dug deeply into the reserves of the little bit of composure she had left, mustered up a painfully false smile, and wheeled around to face the man who had so lately held her in his arms.

Zachary was standing no more than four feet in front of her, the two of them separated only by the narrow width of the counter. He held the cash box lightly in his hands, the roll of tickets balanced on the lid.

"Oh, dear," she trilled in a rather strained voice that she barely recognized, "I did, didn't I? How silly of me." Then, holding out her hands, and offering a silent prayer that he wouldn't see how they were trembling, she took possession of the box and tickets, said, "Thanks a million—bye, now, I really must fly," and skipped off to the safety of her office before Zachary could say another word.

She stopped just inside the door, resting her suddenly warm body against the cool doors of the refrigerator, knowing that she had merely delayed the inevitable. She could issue orders to Sheila that she not be disturbed until—she sniffed aloud at the thought—until old Mrs. Harrison's cows came home. It wouldn't matter. The teenager would be like putty in

Zachary's hands. All females were. Little Jennifer was. *She* was. Getting himself past man-crazy Sheila Bizinski would be a piece of cake to a man like Zachary.

"Hi, again," she heard Zachary say from somewhere above her left ear, and she opened her tightly shut eyes to see him standing in the doorway, one bare forearm resting against the doorjamb as he leaned his body into the room. "Playing hide-and-seek, are we? Strange, you didn't strike me as the type to play games."

Oh, how this man's enjoying himself, Sharon seethed, her cornflower-blue eyes turning as coldly cobalt as midnight snow. Stepping away from the refrigerator, she opened the door and reached behind the large bag of chopped onions for the plastic lettuce crisper, daring—just daring—him to say a single sarcastic word as she transferred the box office receipts to the container and placed it back inside.

Still without uttering a word, she sat down at the small desk to begin counting out the change from the cash box, scribbling the totals on a torn piece of scratch paper someone had used to play several games of tick-tack-toe, all the time fighting the fact of Zachary's presence with every fiber of resistance in her body. Finally, the small job done, she could no longer ignore the fact that the man simply refused to take the hint and *go away*.

Turning around slightly in the chair, she went on the offensive. "You want to double-check my addition?" she challenged. "We don't add up the lettuce crisper until the snack bar closes, but you might want to make sure I didn't miscount the change.''

"Now why would I think a thing like that, Sharon?'' he countered. The look of guileless innocence on his face made her want to throw something at him—maybe a nice, solid roll of quarters.

"You weren't supposed to come here again until tomorrow morning,'' she went on, knowing that somehow, some way, she had to get rid of the man. "You don't play fair.''

"Then we are playing games?'' Zachary asked, cocking one well-defined dark eyebrow at her.

"We aren't. You are. You come barreling in here Friday night like some sort of Attila the Hun on a rampage, treat me as if I remind you of a nagging toothache you once had earlier today when we were on the golf course, and then show up here tonight like some knight riding to the rescue, acting as if your only goal in life was to spend eternity working in a broken-down drive-in that you know darn well you're going to close tomorrow. And that's not even mentioning what you did down at the ticket booth.''

"Oh, come on, Sharon,'' Zachary prompted, with what Sharon considered a rakish leer on his handsome face, "don't quit on me now. By all means, let's mention it. After all, I thought we were getting along famously.''

Suddenly Sharon forgot her embarrassment, forgot the temporary insanity that had her believing that she was—wild as it seemed now—*falling for* the arrogant man standing in front of her, forgot that she had planned to beg, plead and to do everything else she could to save Wheeler's from extinction. She merely reacted.

She slapped her hands sharply against her bare thighs, exposed beneath her red cotton shorts, and then hopped to her feet, saying, "That's it. End of discussion. I have a theater to run, at least for one more night. Mr. St. Clair, I believe you know your way out. Excuse me, please," she apologized abruptly, edging past him quickly with her breath held before jogging across the width of the snack bar toward the safety of the projection booth, then closing the door behind her.

"Denny, you can go outside now and keep an eye on the customers. I'll take over here," she said, taking up her position alongside Gloria Swanson. "Sean's flashlight is on the center island in the snack bar. Don't forget to check the fences; Sean caught three kids trying to sneak in the other night."

Denny and Sam exchanged looks at Sharon's obvious nervousness before the younger man shrugged his shoulders and quietly took his leave. "You'll need to replace Gloria's positive carbon after one more reel, Shari," was all he said as he turned the knob to open the door.

"Oh, Denny, don't go that way. Go out and around the other—"

But Sharon was too late with her warning. The moment the door opened Zachary St. Clair stepped inside the dark booth, his right hand outstretched, calmly asking Sharon to introduce him to the two men. George, now snoring softly, remained out of sight in the corner.

"Good grief!" Zachary exclaimed with a short laugh as the introductions were completed. "I haven't seen projectors like these since I was a kid. Quite the museum pieces, aren't they?"

Sharon bristled yet again, wondering just how the man so instinctively knew where to place his needles. "Gloria Swanson and Veronica Lake aren't spring chickens anymore, but they hold their own," she told him defiantly, reaching out a hand to touch Gloria as if her action could protect the old machine from attack. "Popsie—that is my grandfather, had them installed when this theater was built. They're terrific projectors—they just don't make equipment like this anymore."

"I'll say they don't," Zachary replied, moving forward to inspect Veronica, first from one side, then the other. The projector, which stood about five feet high and half as wide, was made up of three separate parts, a lamp house, a projection head and a sound head, all mounted on a strong metal base that was bolted into the floor. He reached out one hand to touch the side of the projector. "My report said Wheeler's was a carbon house, but I never imagined—"

"Keep your miserable hands off my Veronica!" George ordered, his voice slightly slurred as he lurched to his feet and took a step in Zachary's direction, one clenched fist in the air. "What do you know about anything, huh? You with your newfangled automated 'platter' houses. I know why you're here. Shari told me. You're only interested in putting hardworking men out of their jobs—just so you can make more and more money. Right, Shari?"

"Here now, hold on, old boy," Sharon heard Zachary warn as she watched him reach out to steady George before the man could topple to the floor. Her heart hit her toes as she saw the owner of the St. Clair Theater Corporation wrinkle up his fine, aristocratic nose and exclaim, "Why, you're drunk!"

"Got that in one, smart boy. Darn right I am!" George declared proudly before he slumped, rag doll-like in Zachary's arms.

Everything after that moment would later seem rather hazy for Sharon, as she somehow heard the soft ringing of the warning bell that said a reel change was coming up in one minute. Calling to Sam to keep his eyes open, she ran around the projector to stand beside Gloria, watching the screen intently out the small window, waiting for the cue dot in the corner, which would signal the first change.

When she saw the dot she told Sam to start up Veronica, then counted slowly to ten before the second cue dot appeared and she cut Gloria off. She had fifteen minutes to strip Gloria down, change the lens size for the intermission reel, insert a new carbon in the lamp house and thread up the projector head. Somehow, some way, in that short span of time, she told herself as her hands moved automatically at her tasks, she had to find a way to explain George's actions.

But when she turned around to face the music both Zachary and the projectionist were nowhere in sight.

"Where—where did they go?" she asked Sam, fear coloring her voice. "Are they in my office?"

"Mr. St. Clair said he'd make sure George got home all right," Sam told her as he turned up the projection booth speaker to check on the sound. "I gave him George's house key and directions to the place. Didn't you hear him say goodbye? Mr. St. Clair said he'd meet you here tomorrow morning at eleven. Nice guy, huh, considering George wanted to punch his lights out."

Sharon, one hand to her mouth, sank back against the cool concrete wall and shut her eyes.

Chapter Five

Zachary took his time as he drove the sports car along the narrow back-country roads that led from George Blakeman's small house to Wheeler's Drive-In, rerunning the events of the previous evening in his head. He'd had quite a night, all in all, first with Sharon in the ticket booth, and then later, before falling asleep in George's small living room, going through the man's many scrapbooks that traced back through the years to the late 1930s.

While reading the newspaper clippings, Zachary had learned all about George's close brush with tragedy in a downtown Philadelphia theater, and seen the yellowed pay stub of the projectionist's first paycheck from Wheeler's Drive-In, signed by Sharon's grandfather. It wasn't hard to put two and two together, and it certainly went a long way toward explaining George's problem—and his violent reaction to the

possibility that the drive-in that had become his ref-
uge would finally be shut down.

From thoughts of George, Zachary's mind turned
to the many pictures of Al Wheeler that appeared in
the scrapbooks and the realization that his own father had begun his first indoor theater on just such a
hope and a prayer as Al. Sharon would like Dad; he's
a lot like her grandfather was, he thought again as he
drove along, a rueful smile on his lips. What an op-
erator old Al Wheeler must have been, he decided, remembering the newspaper clipping that told the story
of how the drive-in had begun.

Wheeler, so the story went, had seen an outdoor
movie theater during a visit to Atlantic City, New Jersey in 1933. Inspired, he then returned to Pennsylvania, hung up a big sheet of white cloth between two
tall trees, set up a single loudspeaker in the middle of
an old cornfield and begun showing films to the local
residents.

"And the rest is history," Zachary said aloud in
admiration of the man's daring. "When his only son
sold the business after the old man's death, Sharon
must have been devastated, if all those pictures showing her working alongside her grandfather as she was
growing up meant anything. The drive-in's last two
owners haven't helped my case any, either, considering the way they both let the place go to seed. She and
George have every right to hate my guts."

And that bothered Zachary, it bothered him more
than he liked to admit, even to himself. He liked
George, what little he had gotten to know of the man
through his scrapbooks after he had helped the pro-

jectionist to bed. Earlier that morning, over breakfast, Zachary had realized that George also reminded him of his father, while the man's reminiscences had given him a glimpse of what the theater business must have been like when his father had opened his very first small theater.

Oh, yes, his father had told him stories of the good old days, the days when the projectionists were in their heyday—the heartthrobs of every vaudeville girl—but Zachary hadn't really worked around a theater since the year before he left for college, and the memories had faded under the pressures of building a comfortable business into a multimillion-dollar corporation.

Zachary had even spent a summer running a projector like Veronica, although the dubious "romance" of working with the dangerous, highly flammable nitrate film had passed with the changeover to acetate film just before he was born. During that summer he had struck up a friendship with gruff Charlie Barrows, one of his father's first employees, and the two of them had helped pass the hours on their lengthy ten-hour shifts by trying to best each other on little-known movie trivia.

"Frontiersman Jim Bowie was portrayed by Alan Ladd in *The Iron Mistress*, Sterling Hayden in *The Last Command*, Jeff Morrow in *The First Texan*, and—oh, yes—by Richard Widmark in *The Alamo*," Zachary recited aloud now as he turned onto the main highway and headed for the drive-in. "Damn, but I lost a lot of money to Charlie that summer. But I learned. Boy, how I learned."

A shadow of sadness descended on Zachary then, removing the reminiscent smile from his face as he realized that he had absolutely no idea what had ever happened to Charlie Barrows since that long-ago summer, or if the man was still alive.

Even the theater they had worked in together had changed. It was an automated "platter" house now, with a single manager-projectionist responsible for the three screens that had been carved out of the old single screen building. Silently, he acknowledged that Charlie would never have been able to make the transition to the automated projectors, that a man like Charlie wouldn't even have bothered to try.

"It's not my fault, dammit!" Zachary protested out loud as he turned sharply onto the gravel path that led to the drive-in. "We've progressed to the point where I can run an eight-screen house with two projectionists, not sixteen. It's cost-effective, it's rational, it's the wave of the future."

Driving through the opened gates and onto the lot, Zachary took the time to look at himself in the narrow rearview mirror. "Then why do you feel like such a rat, St. Clair? Why do you feel like apologizing to George, and Charlie—even your dad? And why do you feel like you owe Sharon Wheeler the biggest apology of them all? Answer me that, St. Clair, answer me that!"

Still feeling rather bemused, Sharon was just in the process of hanging up the phone after talking with the thoroughly delighted though slightly hung-over

George Blakeman when she heard Zachary's car pull up behind the snack bar.

Instantly, her heart began to pound almost painfully in her chest. She dug nervously into her purse, hunting for her mirror, just to make sure she still looked passably human after spending a nearly sleepless night, worrying about what she could possibly say to explain away the happenings of the previous night.

But now it wasn't necessary, at least according to George. She heard herself giving out with a quick, nervous giggle as she tried to take it all in. *Wheeler's was going to stay open!* George had just gotten through telling her that Zachary had told him so just that morning while he—the president of the St. Clair Theater Corporation—had served up bacon and eggs to the man who had so lately insulted him before trying to punch him in the nose!

Not only that, George had told her, but Zachary had given the projectionist the week off, telling him to get some rest, while he, Zachary, would take over his duties at the drive-in.

"And he's going to order repairs, Shari. Can you believe that!" the projectionist had fairly yelled into the phone. She had heard the sounds of the old man's grateful tears in his raspy voice. "He said that Wheeler's Drive-In is a part of history and it's up to us to keep that history alive. What a guy! Right?"

"Yes, George. Right," Sharon said now pensively as she rose to go greet her employer. "What a guy. My only question now is—can I really believe his motives are so straightforward? Or am I flattering myself? Am

I simply reading too much into one stolen kiss in the moonlight?''

Oh, Lord, no one man has the right to look that good, especially a man dressed in one of George's faded plaid shirts, Sharon thought as she rounded the side of the snack bar a few moments later to see Zachary, his lean length propped casually against the left front fender of the low slung sports car.

"Hi, there," he said cordially, turning his head in her direction as she slowly approached the car. "I was just standing out here for a moment, admiring the view. There certainly is a lot of countryside out here, isn't there?"

"There usually is, in the country," Sharon responded, cursing herself for being flippant. It was just that she was so nervous! "But we do have several houses behind us that were built some years after the drive-in opened. Popsie always said it was the free speakers that made the people decide to build here."

Zachary turned around to look at the row of ranch homes that all had backyards facing the theater. "Free speakers?" he said, his tone incredulous. "For—let me see—seven houses? With this place barely holding its own? You've got to be kidding."

Nice job, Wheeler, Sharon told herself. *Open mouth, insert foot. Now how do I make Mr. Bottom Line understand?* "Popsie always considered it to be a cheap insurance policy, Mr. St. Clair. In return for the speakers, our neighbors keep a pretty close watch on the place, alerting us to vandalism, or people trying to sneak in under the fence. Don't forget, no one is here all winter long. It's simply one hand washing the other—just like in any business."

"You're right, of course," Zachary agreed to her amazement, smiling at her as he began walking slowly toward the snack bar, "although I wonder just how that little piece of information is going to look in the annual report. You tell me—do we list the cost under insurance, or public relations?"

Sharon lowered her head for a moment in relief, then followed him, saying quickly, "I talked to George this morning and he told me you plan to keep the drive-in open. He also told me how nice you were to him. I—I want to thank you, for—everything."

Zachary stopped just short of the snack bar door, turning around to take hold of her at the shoulders. She looked up into his smiling green eyes as he said, his voice gentle, "Now, that didn't hurt so much, did it, Shari? And you're welcome—*for everything*."

She swallowed hard as her attention was taken by the sensuous long line of Zachary's mouth as it hovered so close to hers, and she wondered yet again if Zachary was beginning to take more than a businessman's impersonal interest in Wheeler's. More than that, she found herself wondering why she hoped his interest was on more of a personal level.

Easy, Wheeler, she quickly told herself, you're not thinking straight again. Determined to bring the discussion back to reality, she rushed on, "I—um—I think I also need to apologize to you. I haven't treated you very well since you got here."

"No, you haven't, have you?" Zachary remarked, his thumbs beginning to lightly massage her shoulders as he gave her a quick glimpse of the long slashing dimples that appeared in his lean, tanned cheeks whenever he smiled. "But—being the heck of a nice guy that I am—I have to tell you that I'm more than willing to let you try to make it up to me."

Sharon, startled by what he might have been implying, quickly stepped back two paces, looking hopefully to the right and left of her as if for assistance before speaking again. "Yes—er—yes, well, I'm sure we'll be able to maintain a reasonably civilized working relationship for the short time you'll be here. George already warned me that—um—that is, George said you told him to take the week off and you'd stand in for him. That wasn't really necessary. The drive-in is closed until Friday, you know, so all that has to be done for the week are a few routine jobs."

She stopped speaking momentarily, trying to get her breath, then continued. "Like policing the grounds, cleaning the snack bar area, packing up *Spy in the Eye* and its co-feature to send back to the distributor, and previewing the weekend films when they come in Friday morning; that sort of thing. I really think—"

"Sounds like fun, Shari," Zachary interrupted her just as she thought she was losing her mind, babbling on and on as if she had actually been flustered beyond coherence by his last, fairly suggestive statement. After all, she was almost twenty-five years old, and it wasn't as if she had never been propositioned before—*if* that was what had just happened.

"Good grief—er, that is, good, *good*!" she amended hastily. "I just thought you ought to know what you're letting yourself in for, that's all," she then ended fatalistically, nodding her head rapidly as if glad that everything was settled.

"Just tell me what to do first. I'm so unused to taking a vacation that a working vacation might be just what the doctor ordered."

Sharon looked at Zachary for a long moment, then spread her arms wide and shrugged, figuring she might as well go along with him. "In that case, I'll bow to your wishes, Mr. St. Clair. You'll find the plastic bags and shovels in a corner of the storage shed next to the front gate. George usually starts in the last row and works his way forward. I've already got *Spy in the Eye* packed up and ready to go, so the cleanup detail is next on his list of chores."

Zachary looked around the sprawling three-hundred car theater grounds, which were littered with discarded paper cups, crumpled hot dog wrappers, popcorn buckets and small bits of food that were providing a meal for several dozen birds, which were at the moment picking their way through the debris. "You're kidding, right? I mean, you don't really expect me to play *janitor*?"

"Why not?" Sharon asked, her tongue firmly in her cheek, taking a small slice of satisfaction out of knowing that the tables had been turned just a little. "After all, I'm management—after a fashion. You couldn't actually believe *I* would assign myself such a menial, disgusting job. Besides," she added, already walking away, "then I wouldn't have time for my very favorite job of all—cleaning the bathrooms."

"Over my dead body!" she heard Zachary shout, and turned back to see him standing right behind her, his handsome face revealing the fact that he was absolutely furious. "There's no way in bloody hell I'll see you cleaning bathrooms."

Sharon could feel herself bristling at his arrogance. "Is that right? Well, then, what do you suggest? I hire a cleaning service? You already said Wheeler's is barely breaking even. How do you think we've lasted this long, if I hadn't found some way to cut a few of the costs? Grow up, St. Clair. This isn't some plush and mahogany boardroom, this is the real world. And in the real world people have to clean bathrooms."

She stood very still as she waited for his reaction. They were back to square one, she thought sadly, knowing that only moments ago he had been ready to take her in his arms. *Now,* she told herself ruefully, *all he wants is to shake me silly. I get the feeling this is going to be the shortest working relationship in history.*

After silently deciding that she had somehow destroyed something she really wasn't sure had even existed, Sharon could not hide her astonishment when Zachary at last announced evenly, "Very well then, boss, clean bathrooms if you want. But *I'll* take care of the men's bathroom, if it's all the same to you. In return, we can split up the garbage detail. Deal?"

Sharon looked warily at his outstretched hand, wondering if she could possibly have heard him correctly. Then slowly, hesitantly, she held out her own right hand. "Deal."

As soon as she felt his warm hand clasp hers, she knew she was lost. It took only the slightest tug on his part to pull her completely into his arms, and the bar-

gain, begun in anger, was sealed with a most satisfying kiss.

If you were smart, Zachary lectured himself as he
made his way up aisle seven, a halfful plastic bag in
one hand, a shovel in the other, *you'd get back in your
car and drive away from this place as fast as you can.
You haven't done anything this stupid to get to first
base with a woman since the third grade, when you
hung upside down from the monkey bars to get
Maryjo Handley's attention.*

"My arm was in a cast for six weeks," he said out
loud, putting down the bag in order to wield the shovel
on a small mountain of garbage that seemed to be at-
tracting more than its share of flying insects in the
early-afternoon sunshine. "It sure was a lot easier
cleaning up the aisles in Dad's theaters. At least I
didn't have to worry about getting stung."

Just as if the thought had conjured up the deed,
Zachary suddenly felt a sharp, stinging sensation on
the back of his neck. He dropped the shovel and began slapping furiously at his face and upper body, as
if to ward off any further attack, then began walking
in carefully controlled haste toward the sports car
parked behind the snack bar. "Sharon!" he called out
as he walked. "I've been stung. I might need some
help."

Sharon, who had been working her way along the
third row of parking ramps, looked up in time to see
Zachary opening the passenger door of his car and
climbing inside. "Hey!" she called as she stripped off
the thin latex gloves she always wore when working

around the grounds and started in the direction of the car. "I couldn't quite hear what you said, but if it has anything to do with taking a coffee break, I'm all for it. Gosh, but it's hot."

"I'm not resting, Sharon," Zachary told her as she reached the open car door. "I've been stung."

Ah, poor baby, Sharon thought, raising one bare forearm to push an errant lock of honey-blond hair back away from her forehead. Aloud, she taunted, "Oh, ye of the faint heart! Don't tell me you're going to give up just because of a little bee sting? There's always a lot of bees around here—they're attracted to the soda and bits of candy, all the sweet stuff."

"That's me, all right," Zachary said, surprising her by his apparent breathlessness. "Sweet stuff. Dammit. Why can't I get this blasted thing open?"

Sharon stood up very straight for a moment as the shock brought on by her realization of just what might be happening finally hit her. Quickly dropping to her knees beside the open car door, she looked inside to see Zachary struggling to open a small black case. Beads of perspiration stood out on his forehead and upper lip.

"Here," she ordered, reaching out her hand, "give me that. You sit still, okay?"

Zachary let go of the case without protest, then reached up to rub at the front of his throat. "I—I'm allergic."

"Yes, I may not be an Einstein, but I think I've figured that out," Sharon told him as she opened the case and looked at the small syringe that lay inside. "Are you having trouble breathing?"

"A little. I think my throat is getting tight, but—but sometimes just the thought of what could happen is enough to give—symptoms. Damn, I'm getting dizzy. Better hurry. Before I start seeing double."

Sharon could feel the burning-cold heat of panic racing through her veins. Zachary looked awful, his exposed skin beginning to take on a mottled appearance and purplish blotches marring the smooth skin of his throat. She lifted the syringe holding its premeasured dose of medication from the case and gingerly held it out to him. "Here, take it," she ordered, fighting her lifelong fear of needles. "You'd better hurry—you don't look so good."

Zachary was literally gasping for breath now. She watched him open his eyes and stare at the needle as if he was having trouble focusing on it. "Sick to my stomach. Can't see. Can't do it."

"You have to do it!" Sharon fairly screamed. "I don't know what to do. Don't you have to have the shot as soon as possible?"

"Twenty—twenty minutes," Zachary gasped. "Hospital."

The nearest hospital was more than twenty minutes away, and more than five minutes had passed since Zachary had been stung. Sharon pressed her fist to her mouth, more frightened than she had ever been in her life. "This is no time to be playing Miss Faint Heart," she then told herself bracingly, purposely looking straight at the syringe. "Zachary, listen to me. You'll have to give yourself the shot. Now tell me how I can help!"

"Alcohol wipe," he told her, shakily pointing toward the case and the small, white flat packet still lying inside. "Rub it on the side of my arm, the fleshiest part."

Get hold of yourself, Wheeler, she instructed herself silently as she completed the task.

"Tell me what to do next," Sharon said as she quickly rubbed the alcohol-saturated swab roughly against his arm.

Zachary raised his head and blinked twice, looking at the syringe she now held in her right hand. "The needle," he croaked. "Uncover the needle."

Stupid! Sharon berated herself, carefully wiping her left hand on her shorts before pulling off the small plastic cover and exposing the short, wickedly thin needle. "Oh, my God," she breathed, swallowing hard as a wave of nausea rolled over her.

"Now hand it to me," Zachary was telling her. "And turn your head. I don't want you fainting on me."

Sharon gingerly handed him the syringe, then followed his advice and turned her head. After all, it wouldn't look good for the patient to recover while the nurse faded away at his feet.

"Do you want some more water?" Sharon asked ten minutes later, taking the empty paper cup from Zachary, who was still sitting in the front seat of the sports car. He looked so much better now—she could see that by both his color and the fact that his hands had finally stopped shaking—but she couldn't help but wish he'd agree to go to the hospital for a checkup.

"I'm fine, Sharon," Zachary assured her, turning slightly in the car seat as if he was about to get up. "I told you, the adrenaline works very quickly. Another couple of minutes and you'd never know I was stung. I'll follow up the shot with antihistamine pills later if I feel the need, but the worst is over. I have to admit, though, that I wasn't feeling too thrilled a few minutes ago. It's been a long time between stings, and I didn't think I'd react so violently."

Still squatting on the ground beside the open car door, Sharon slowly crumpled the cup and placed it carefully on the ground. "So you're just fine?" she said evenly. "Good. Very good. Because now I have another question for you."

She took a deep breath and then fairly shouted, *"Why didn't you tell me you're allergic to bee stings, you ridiculous man!* Dammit, Zachary, you scared me half to death! I never would have allowed you to do the stupid job if you had told me what could happen."

Zachary sank back again against the soft leather seat. "You care, Sharon. How nice. It almost makes the whole thing worth it."

"Of course I care! Don't go reading anything into that, Zachary St. Clair. I'd care just as much if it happened to anybody—George, Denny, Sam—*anybody*! Besides, even if it wasn't really terrific for you to be lying there, sweating and shaking all over the place, it sure as heck didn't make my day, either. I thought I might have to go jabbing that needle into you."

"I guess we can just thank heaven for little favors, Shari," he soothed, stroking her cheek with his right hand. "As it is, with luck, I may even play the violin again some day."

Sharon's eyelids narrowed as she glared at the man who had so recently scared her half to death. "That's it, make a joke of the whole thing!"

Sharon didn't know what else she could have said if he had given her the chance, because suddenly she felt her body being pulled unceremoniously across his in the front seat. She looked up to see Zachary's face just inches above her own and all her fear, all her indignation, melted under his hot, green gaze.

"All I want to do is thank you for possibly saving my life, Sharon Wheeler. Why don't you be a good girl, and just accept my thanks gracefully?"

"You—you're welcome," Sharon heard herself squeak as the intimacy of their position turned her bones to water. He was going to kiss her, she just knew it. He had kissed her before—twice—but she instinctively knew that this time it would be different. This kiss wasn't going to either be stolen, like his first kiss Friday night, or playful, like the one they had shared just an hour earlier.

Oh, no. Zachary was demanding her full cooperation in this kiss, she could see it in his eyes, and her recent, fairly intimate acquaintance with his lean attractive body fueled her imagination with possibilities she could not—did not want to—ignore.

"But I didn't really thank you yet, Shari," she heard him saying as she concentrated on the enticing movements of his mouth as he spoke. "Still, it's nice to know I'm 'welcome.'"

Oh, Lord, this man does things to me that couldn't possibly be legal, Sharon thought, struggling to keep her composure as she realized that somehow, without her explicit instructions, her arms had wound themselves betrayingly around his neck. "That—that's not what I meant. I can understand what you're thinking—at least I think so—but I didn't really mean that you're—well, maybe I did—but not *really* wel come—"

The whole time she had been speaking, rambling actually, Sharon had been acutely aware of Zachary's hands, which were molding and shaping themselves to the contours of her back, and his legs, which formed such a warm, suggestive cradle for her body. "You— you're just feeling grateful, that's all," she told him, trying to reason away the almost hungry look she saw in his green eyes. "You're just not yourself yet. I really think you ought to go back to your hotel and—"

He didn't let her get any further. She had been faintly disappointed that he had even let her get as far as she had. But finally, unable to stifle the satisfied sigh that escaped her slightly parted lips, she felt the gentle firmness of his mouth against hers.

The loudest on-screen kiss took place between Jack Palance and Shelley Winters in *I Died a Thousand Times*, Sharon thought, unbidden. The longest screen kiss took place between—oh, Lord, who cares!

She forced herself to remain motionless for a few moments, to savor the warmth and texture of Zachary's mouth as he moved his lips slowly against hers, then retreated, then suckled first her top, and then her full lower lip, his moist tongue lightly tracing a sanity-destroying circle on her soft, inner flesh.

But when she thought he was really drawing away from her, Sharon moved forward slightly, reluctant to end the embrace. His reaction to her switch to the initiative, which wasn't long in coming, sent her spiraling helplessly into a mindless whirl of ecstasy. She was crushed tightly against his body, her mouth feeding from his, her hands exploring new territories he opened to her, her heartbeats racing in time with his.

Sharon didn't know where it would end, didn't care where it would end—didn't want it to end. Her entire universe had narrowed; to this car, this man, this glorious feeling.

She wasn't kissing the St. Clair Theater Corporation, or her profit-conscious boss, or even the rescuer who had so lately given Wheeler's Drive-In a new lease on life.

She was kissing the man of the laughing green eyes, the man who flirted with pigtailed little girls, the man who fed George Blakeman bacon and eggs, the man who had argued with her, infuriated her, intrigued her and occupied her every thought since he had first appeared in her life.

And she would go on kissing him, holding him, loving him, until this spectacular scene had reached its culmination, until the credits had all run by, even after the screen had gone blank and the world had faded away.

Chapter Six

Sharon. Shari, honey," Zachary whispered into her ear as he pressed her head against his chest. "Someone's coming."

No! They wouldn't dare! Sharon clutched her arms even tighter about Zachary's waist as she fought to bring herself back to reality. But then she heard it too, the soft crunching sound of rubber tires moving along the gravel path toward the snack bar. She felt like a teenager caught in the back seat of a parked car, as she rapidly pulled herself out of his arms, tucking her T-shirt back down into the waistband of her shorts as she spied the delivery truck heading directly for the space next to the sports car.

She looked at Zachary, on whose lap she still rested, her bare legs hanging outside the opened car door, and realized that he was just as upset by their unexpected visitor as she was. "Just—just like in the movies," she heard herself saying. "The timely interruption. That's how they keep their PG ratings. Though I don't ever remember the interruption taking the form of the propane gas man. I didn't know Gary was coming today."

She tried to extricate herself from her compromising position, earning Zachary's rather painfully uttered "Take it easy, Shari, I'm not a well man at the moment," for her troubles.

Then, still pushing at her disheveled hair, and with a becoming flush of pink still riding high on her cheeks, she walked rapidly over to the edge of the grass parking area to greet Gary, the deliveryman, noticing out of the corner of her eye that Zachary was also out of the car and heading for the snack bar.

Fifteen minutes later, just enough time for Gary to complete his delivery and leave—and more than enough time for Sharon to realize exactly what had almost happened in the front seat of Zachary's sports car—she walked into the coolness of the snack bar to see her boss sitting in *her* office, inspecting the account book.

"He's gone," she said nervously, leaning against the doorjamb. "Would you like some ice cream? We've got plenty."

If she had been nervous before, she was doubly apprehensive once Zachary turned around to face her, for he had that forbidding, closed look on his face that he had worn the night Gertrude had invaded the drive-in. "Sharon, you said you weren't expecting that deliveryman. How would he have gotten in here if you weren't here? Don't you lock the gates?"

Instantly Sharon was on the defensive. She should have known better than to think that scene in the car had really changed anything—that any of Zachary's recent actions had changed anything. Scratch a businessman like Zachary and you'll find a profit and loss statement under his skin. "Of course I lock the gates!" she was stung into answering. "What do you think I am—stupid?"

"Then I repeat my question. How would Gary have been able to make his delivery if you weren't here?"

Sharon looked down at the toe of her sneaker as she absently kicked at a loose corner of the linoleum. "He—he has a key," she told him reluctantly, waiting for the explosion that she knew wouldn't be long in coming. "So do the dairyman, the restaurant supply man, the meter man and the butcher. Popsie always said it was easier to do that than to always be running out here in the middle of the week to let them—"

"I don't give a flying fig what your Popsie said!" Zachary shouted at her, slamming the accounts book shut and rising to his feet to stare down at her. "Don't you read *Reel People*, or any of the trade magazines? There are pirates out there stealing movie prints left, right and center, then selling them for videos, or overseas."

"Now just a minute. Just a darn minute! If you're insinuating that—"

"We're responsible for the films we're showing, and you—you give every Tom, Dick and *Gary* a damn *key* to the place! Woman, do you have any head for business at all—or are you only concerned with keeping in a good supply of sauerkraut for your damned hot dogs?''

So much for worrying about telling him you're not that kind of girl, Wheeler, she told herself, feeling herself beginning to shake with fury. Romance seems to be the last thing on his mind. Well, if it's a fight he wants, I'm sure not going to disappoint him!

Sharon shoved out her firm chin and jabbed a finger repeatedly into Zachary's chest as she answered his accusations, her belligerence lending a warning note of sharpness to her voice. ''I am fully aware of the warnings issued by the Motion Picture Association, Mr. St. Clair, as are all Wheeler employees. That projection room is locked at both entrances every moment it's unoccupied, and the films are all kept under separate lock and key to boot. I couldn't care less about your poor opinion of our snack bar, but I would like to go on record as saying I do resent very much your insinuation that Wheeler's has anything to do with the print piracy going on in the industry. How dare you make such an accusation!''

''I dare, *Miss Wheeler*,'' Zachary growled at her, pushing her accusing finger away as he took another short step in her direction, ''because this theater, for my sins, is now a part of the St. Clair Theater Corporation. It is Wheeler's Drive-In no longer. And I am going to haul this place—kicking and screaming all the way, I'm sure—into the present, *with or without your help.*

''And that, if you are still unclear as to what I have in mind, means that in the future there is going to be a person on duty here at all times—not just when it won't interfere with your friendly little golf dates.''

"How dare you—''

Zachary went on as if she hadn't spoken. "That means that the only keys to the gates will be in the hands of authorized personnel, period. It means that—that sauerkraut will no longer be on the menu, dammit. Now get on the phone and find somebody to come out here and clean this place up! You're the manager—for the moment. I suggest you start acting like one." He then reached out his hand and gestured toward her T-shirt and shorts. "And for God's sake, don't you own a skirt?''

Sharon abruptly closed her mouth, as she belatedly realized that it had dropped open the moment Zachary had begun his tirade. Then she hurried after his departing back. "Just where do you think you're going?" she called to him as he slammed his way out the snack bar door. "You shouldn't be driving yet, you idiot!''

"Why not?" Zachary hurled at her over his shoulder. "You have more surprises in store for me? Perhaps you want to tell me that you also gave gate keys to the entire Vienna Boys' Choir? Please, I don't think I could take any more today.''

"Very funny," Sharon told him in a tone that said she didn't think he had been funny at all. "It's just that it hasn't been that long since you were stung. It might not be safe. The last thing I need is to have your untimely death on my hands. I doubt there would be a jury in the world who would believe I hadn't killed you!''

Zachary stopped, then turned around for only a moment, looking her up and down in a way that had her involuntarily taking one step backward. "It's a damn sight safer than staying here with you," she heard him say before he was off again, his angry strides taking him rapidly out of sight. "I'll be back tomorrow at noon to check on your progress. Be here."

"You're the Scotch guy. I remember," the hotel bartender said jovially that evening as he approached the end of the bar where Zachary sat staring blankly into the mirror above the back bar. "You ever get in that game of golf?"

Zachary looked across the width of the bar at the man, who was placing a short glass containing an inch and a half of amber liquid in front of him. "Yes, yes I did. Thank you, er—"

"Stosh," the bartender supplied eagerly. "Stanley Wojewodzki, actually, but everybody calls me Stosh. It's easier. You?"

It's Mudd—with two Ds, Zachary almost said, then realized Stosh didn't deserve his sarcasm. "Zachary," he told the man. "Are you from around here, Stosh, or did you come to Allentown to work in the hotel?"

"Me?" Stosh answered, whipping out a damp cloth to wipe at the already shiny surface of the bar. "Nah, I'm a local—lived here all my life. No big cities like Philly or New York for me. Allentown's got it all, you know. You've got your shopping malls, your good schools, your nice housing—"

"Do you go to the movies, Stosh?" Zachary heard himself asking, wondering why he was interested.

Stosh nodded his head vigorously. "Oh, sure. Me and the wife go every Saturday night like clockwork. Wouldn't miss it. This is a big movie town."

"Indoor theaters, of course," Zachary prodded, nodding his head in agreement, already knowing that the theater market in the district that included eastern Pennsylvania, southern New Jersey, and Delaware was one of the most profitable in the country. After all, why else had he invested in the area?

"Oh, sure, but only in the wintertime, when Wheeler's Drive-In isn't open. I've heard a rumor that the old place has been sold again and the new owner might shut it down. That would be a darn shame. The wife is sort of partial to Wheeler's, and the kids like it. It's okay by me, too, because it's cheap. And the food! Hey, you've got your steak sandwiches, your hot dogs, your nachos, your—"

"Yes, yes," Zachary cut in before Stosh could recite the entire menu, "I've heard Wheeler's is a nice place. It would be a shame to see it closed down."

He watched as the bartender smiled reminiscently. "Me and the wife—we met there, you know. 'Course, that was three kids ago. Now we even watch the movie," he said, winking, "if you know what I mean!"

Had the entire population of Allentown met and married thanks to Wheeler's Drive-In? First Sharon had told him about Denny, the employee who worked in the ticket booth, and now Stosh was telling him the same thing about himself. *Maybe that's what's be-*

hind my moment of madness this afternoon with Sharon, Zachary told himself, looking for any excuse with which he could comfort himself. There must be something in the air out there.

"Hey, I guess you didn't want Scotch tonight, huh?" Stosh suggested, interrupting Zachary's thoughts. "You haven't touched your drink. You can have something else, you know. We've got your beer, your wine, your—"

Zachary hastily lifted his glass and took a drink, the fiery liquid stinging the back of his throat and sending a reviving jolt of liquid warmth through his body. "The Scotch is fine, Stosh. I guess I'm just tired. I think I'll make it an early evening." He finished off the drink, stood up and reached a hand into his pants pocket. "What's the damage?"

The bartender held out his hands and smiled. "Hey, keep your money in your pocket. You're a visitor to our fair city. This one's on me."

Zachary thanked the man, then made sure to leave a sizable tip at the other end of the bar before making for the lobby and the elevator that would take him to his room on the fourth floor of the downtown hotel. But the smile Stosh's antics had put on his face faded as Zachary unlocked the door to his room and faced the dark emptiness that waited on the other side.

After stripping off the suit he had donned earlier and climbing into the running shorts that were the closest thing to pajamas he would wear, even while traveling around the country to visit his business holdings, Zachary stretched himself out full length on the king-size bed, his arms at his sides, as he stared up at the ceiling.

Lifting his right hand after a moment, he began absently rubbing at the site where he had injected the adrenaline. "It's good I could use the needle myself," he said aloud in the empty room. "As it is, I'll probably be black and blue for a week."

If that were the only place I've been bruised, I might still have been able to walk away from this town with no regrets, he thought, abruptly rising from the bed to walk over to the window and look down on the street below.

But, no. Sharon Wheeler had left her mark all over him, whether he wanted to acknowledge that fact or not. She and George had already sent him on one guilt trip by showing him that he'd somehow lost sight of the theaters and the people who work in them. They may have done him a favor in the long run, he thought, because a good businessman has to remember where he's been, if he is to keep some perspective on the future.

But Zachary knew he could not convince himself that it was only a few good memories of the past—of his years spent listening to his father's reminiscences, of his summer spent working with Charlie Barrows in that glorious old Art Deco theater in Buffalo—that had somehow resulted in his decision to keep Wheeler's open. His motives were much more involved, much more closely connected with his awareness of Sharon Wheeler as a desirable female, than he would like to admit.

What had begun that first night as an infuriating awareness of her strange effect on him had mushroomed that Sunday at the golf course when he found himself ready to punch poor unsuspecting Hugh Kingsley in the mouth for daring to kiss Sharon in his presence.

Lifting his arms to push his fingers wearily through his dark hair before sliding his hands down the back of his neck to begin massaging his aching shoulders, Zachary felt the sharp sting of guilt yet again as he silently acknowledged that he had deliberately set out to seduce one Miss Sharon Wheeler, using his power of life and death over Wheeler's as a shortcut through her defenses.

"You are despicable, and conniving, and everything else Sharon called you," he berated himself aloud, turning away from the window. "You were tired, burned out and looking for a change when you got to town. You took one look at Sharon Wheeler, were attracted to the girl and then deliberately used charm and personality to take what you wanted from her without a thought to the damage you might be doing to an innocent young woman.

"Then, this afternoon, when you realized you were getting in over your head, actually beginning to feel something more than mere physical desire for her, you took the first opportunity you could to lash out at her, wield your almighty power over her head. You're a real gem, St. Clair, you really are."

Dropping heavily onto the bed, Zachary put his head in his hands as he let the full weight of what he had done sink in for the first time. "So far today I've committed myself to keeping Wheeler's open, and I've succeeded in making the first woman I've ever been in danger of seriously caring for hate the sight of me. Now I've got less than a week to turn Wheeler's into a money-making proposition I can defend to the stockholders and—most importantly—to win Sharon Wheeler."

His head popped up suddenly as a thought hit him—as something very near to divine inspiration sent a flash of new strength coursing through his weary body. "Of course!" he exclaimed in elation, leaping to his feet in order to pace rapidly up and down the room. "It's perfect, absolutely perfect! Why didn't I think of this before!"

He fairly ran to the nightstand to pick up the phone. As he dialed the long distance number he laughed aloud, raising his eyes to the ceiling as he said, "If this works, all I'll have to do is find some way to make Sharon want me as much as I want her. And, by God, I do *want* her!"

Sharon walked around to the rear of the snack bar and dumped the bucket of soapy water onto a small patch of weeds that had sprung up through some gaps in the gravel pathway. It had taken her all morning, but the snack bar was spotless, from the projection room floor to the mirrors in the restrooms.

She had not given a second thought to Zachary's angry demand that she hire someone to clean the theater. She wanted to—had to—do it herself. It had been a labor of love.

Returning the bucket to its place in the small shed that stood next to the ticket booth, she then began walking slowly back toward the snack bar for what would be her final visit, mentally calculating how long it would take her to write out her resignation and be off the premises.

She had been able to keep her thoughts at bay throughout the time she had been cleaning and sorting and scrubbing, but now there was nothing else left to be done, nothing left to delay the inevitable.

It was time to say goodbye.

Just the thought of what she had to do brought helpless tears to her eyes, and she stopped in the middle of the third row and looked around at the open-air theater one last time. There was not a single bit of debris left anywhere on the grounds; she had stayed until dusk the night before, policing the area as if she were readying the place for inspection by some commanding officer.

But that wasn't what she was looking at now.

Now she was looking at memories.

Like the time Popsie had spent an entire summer afternoon convincing the five-year-old Sharon that the sliding board located in the small playground at the foot of the movie screen was great fun. "And then he had had to spend the rest of the day trying to convince me to *stop* sliding down the silly thing," she reminisced aloud, smiling a little in spite of her sad mood.

Looking back toward the wooden shed that served as the ticket booth, Sharon remembered the night a huge camper had pulled onto the grounds and the top of the vehicle had slammed into the roof of the booth, turning the entire structure nearly sideways on its cement base. What a night that had been, with the patron screaming about the damage to his camper and Popsie having a fit because the camper was blocking the entrance and he was losing business.

In the end, she recalled, Sharon's grandfather had gone from car to car, enlisting the aid of every high school football player he could find, and the ticket booth had been shoved back into place. "It's still just the least bit crooked," she said now, tilting her head to one side as she looked fondly at the wooden shelter.

"And then there was Errol Flynn," Sharon said, her voice breaking slightly as she remembered her grandfather's old German shepherd, Popsie's constant companion. Errol had been part pet, part watchdog, and he could always be found lying on the grass in front of the box office until the last car of the night had pulled through the gates. Many people had stopped to admire the handsome animal on their way into the theater, but one incident in particular stood out in her mind.

She laughed aloud as she remembered the night she had been helping her grandfather in the booth as an older woman had driven up, stopping her car for a full minute to admire Errol before finally driving up to purchase her ticket.

"What a beautiful dog!" the old lady had gushed, and Sharon could not help but notice that the woman's admiration for Errol seemed to extend to her grandfather, who had always been a handsome man. "Whose is it?"

"Mine," Sharon had heard her grandfather growl, clearly not in the mood for any romantic dalliance.

"Oh, aren't you lucky?" the lady had pushed on, even though Sharon's grandfather had already handed her both her change and her ticket. "Does he always lie there?"

"Yep," Popsie had answered shortly, already looking through the front window of the booth as the line of cars got longer.

"Really? How lovely," the woman had gushed girlishly. "Whatever does he do there?"

"He's keeping a count on the cars for me," Popsie had gritted, throwing his giggling granddaughter a broad wink.

Sharon wiped at the tears now on her cheeks as she recalled the delighted expression that had come over the woman's face at her grandfather's ridiculous explanation.

"Really!" she had heard the woman exclaim delightedly, looking back toward Errol, who had just then been in the middle of a huge doggie yawn. "Isn't that wonderful!" the silly woman had exclaimed, much impressed with Errol's canine abilities, before at last driving away, leaving Sharon and her grandfather holding on to each other, dissolved in laughter.

"Oh, Popsie, how I loved those times," Sharon said into the silence of the vacant theater lot. "Leaving this place is going to be like having to say goodbye to you all over again. But I have to go. I would only be fighting a losing battle if I stayed. Nothing will really ever be the same anymore, not with the St. Clair Theater Corporation turning the place into one of its nondescript clones. I don't think I could bear to watch that, be a part of it. I just don't think I can fight anymore."

Suddenly Sharon heard the sound of an approaching car on the gravel pathway, and for a moment she thought that she had left her departure too late. Seeing Zachary St. Clair again would deplete the last of her reserves, and she'd end up making a complete fool of herself. "He'd misunderstand completely—think I'm leaving because of him. Because he kissed me. Because I kissed him back. Because he hates me. And that's not true," she told the speaker poles that stood along the aisles like sentries at attention. "It's the farthest thing from the truth I ever heard."

That's good, now tell us another one. The dark-faced speaker boxes seemed to mock her, and Sharon turned to run for the snack bar away from her three hundred silent accusers, away from the approaching car bringing Zachary St. Clair back into her life just long enough to remind her of exactly how empty that life would be without him.

"Hey, Shari! Where's the fire?"

She stopped running, relief flooding through her as she recognized the voice of her old friend. "Hugh!" she cried out, turning to see the hotel owner's midnight-blue Chrysler convertible pulling up beside her. "What in the world are you doing all the way out here? Don't tell me your mother sent you."

"Cheeky female," Hugh Kingsley chided, waving Sharon away from the door so that he could open it.

"I never should have told you about Mother's little fantasy. You're getting a swelled head. Maybe that's why you forgot our lunch date today at the club. You were just exercising your power over me. Well, here I am, come begging. Are you happy now?"

Sharon clapped a hand to her mouth in dismay. "Oh, Hugh, I'm so sorry! I was going to meet you, wasn't I? I completely forgot."

Hugh shook his head in mock dejection. "You could have said you were busy, Shari. That I could stand. But to *forget* me? I'm wounded to the quick. But I guess I wouldn't be honest if I said I was surprised. I checked the register at the hotel this morning, and Casanova is still in residence."

"Casanova?"

"Zachary St. Clair. Our handsome captain of industry *is* making a move on you, isn't he? I'd be jealous, but from the way he was looking at you on Sunday, I'd say his intentions are honest."

"Oh, Hugh!" Sharon wailed, then hurled herself into her friend's comforting arms, to cry as she had not cried since she had lost Popsie six years earlier.

Chapter Seven

Zachary woke very early that morning, eager to rush over to Sharon's house as soon as possible to share his good news with her, but he was being frustrated at every turn.

Her phone number and address were not listed in the telephone directory, and repeated calls to George Blakeman's house went unanswered. Zachary chafed at the knowledge, but there was nothing for him to do but wait until closer to noon, and then meet her at Wheeler's as planned.

As he lay back against the propped-up pillows on the bed in the midst of his elation at his brilliance, he slowly began to feel a few niggling doubts creeping unbidden into his mind.

He could dazzle Sharon with his news only if—and it was a big if—she planned on obeying the order he had flung at her so nastily yesterday afternoon. "How could you have been such an idiot as to yell at her that way yesterday? Some genius you are, St. Clair!'' he berated himself aloud. He wouldn't be the least bit surprised if he arrived at the drive-in to find that she was nowhere to be found. Even worse, he knew he couldn't blame her!

"And you don't have the slightest idea where to find her if she doesn't show up at the theater! She could live on the moon for all you know. You've been so busy planning Sharon's future, you haven't taken the time to learn anything at all about her. Talk about your chauvinists, St. Clair. You really take the prize!'' he continued as he rose from the bed and headed for the bathroom.

Zachary's elation at having satisfactorily resolved the problem of Wheeler's Drive-In might have temporarily banished thoughts of his latest argument with Sharon from his mind last night, but this morning's enforced cooling-off period before he could meet with her was rapidly chilling his good mood even more effectively than the cold shower he stood under for ten minutes, trying to marshal his thoughts.

Once dressed and down in the dining room, Zachary pushed his sausage and eggs aimlessly around his plate as he waited for the long morning to end, all his actions of the previous day playing again in his mind, like a bad movie he had been forced to sit through twice.

Not that he regretted their interlude in the front seat of the car, for he didn't. As a matter of fact, he found himself feeling almost grateful to the bee that had sacrificed its little life in the name of romance.

It was his asinine performance— "Yes, St. Clair, asinine," he told himself bitterly fifteen minutes before noon as he finally rounded the corner to drive through the open theater gates—after Gary, the gas man, had left that were giving him second thoughts about how Sharon would take the news he had for her today.

He'd have to handle his explanation very carefully, explain it all in great detail so that she understood that what he was doing was for the best—the only possible solution that was fair to everybody involved. He owed it to his stockholders, he owed it to Sharon and George and the rest of the Wheeler employees.

Mostly, he thought guiltily, *I owe it to myself—because, if I don't handle this exactly right, I just might not escape this place today in one piece.*

Smiling a little as he turned the sports car down the pathway behind the snack bar, his green eyes narrowed a little as he spotted the dark blue convertible parked beside Sharon's compact station wagon.

"Probably just some girlfriend who stopped in for a visit," he consoled himself, eyeing the expensive-looking automobile warily as he climbed out of his own car. "Control yourself, man," he warned under his breath. "You're beginning to act like you've posted no-trespassing signs on the woman."

But no matter what Zachary told himself, no matter whether or not he viewed himself as being a civilized man, nothing could keep his hands from bunching into fists at his sides when he saw the customized license plate as he walked behind the convertible.

" 'KING-1,' " he growled. "Hugh Kingsley! Damn it! How dare she allow her boyfriend to visit her at work? She knew I wanted to talk to her today—*demanded* to meet with her today. Does she think she needs reinforcements—that I'm some kind of monster?"

Zachary's well-intentioned, carefully rehearsed-under-a-cold-shower speech went winging off into oblivion as he strode purposefully around the snack bar to the side door, which stood open in the warm noon air. He stepped inside the doorway, his eyes taking a moment to adjust to the dim light inside before he saw the touching scene that was being played out in front of him.

Sharon, clad once more in T-shirt and shorts, was sitting propped atop the snack bar counter, her bare legs dangling a good two feet above the floor, her honey-blond hair hanging in a molten mass on either side of her woebegone little face as Hugh Kingsley, dressed with a casual elegance that suited his lean frame, hovered over her solicitously, unfolded handkerchief at the ready.

"Now doesn't this make a pretty picture," Zachary fairly snarled as he advanced farther into the room. "Wait! Don't tell me. Let me guess. Cinderella's got a bit of smut in her eye, and Prince Charming has volunteered to get it out for her. Well, don't look now, but the wicked stepmother—or in this case, boss—has just shown up to throw a monkey wrench into the happily-ever-after plot. Too bad, isn't it, Kingsley, and just when you looked like you were getting someplace. Or am I wrong, and I've come in on the last reel, too late to see the love scene?''

"I said, I don't wish to discuss it!" Sharon picked up the five rolls of wrapped bathroom tissue one by one, quickly jamming three of them into the crook of her left arm before barreling out of the office and past Zachary, threatening him with the two rolls of tissue she brandished in front of his face like a weapon as she went.

"All right, all right," Zachary compromised, trotting after her as she slipped neatly under the cut-out section of the Formica bar and lightly skipped outside. "We won't discuss it."

"You're being redundant, St. Clair. I've already said that," Sharon shot at him, breaking into a run.

Vaulting over the bar rather than struggling to bend his tall frame under it, Zachary picked up some ground on her retreating form, but she was still three paces ahead of him as she rounded the corner of the snack bar and headed for the women's rest room. "We won't discuss it," he called after her yet again. "Heaven knows I'd just as soon forget the whole thing ever happened. But, please, Shari, at least be fair enough to let me apologize for what I said."

"Oh, sure. How like a man! Now you want to shift all the responsibility to *my* shoulders, just because I won't let you soothe your conscience with a quick apology. You do all the damage with that overdeveloped imagination of yours, and then a simple 'I'm sorry' is supposed to fix everything? Well, you can just forget it! I don't know how I'll ever be able to face Hugh again.''

"In that case, I withdraw my apology," Zachary called after her. "In fact, now I'm *glad* I did it!"

After Hugh—still smiling like some demented Cheshire cat—had left her to fend for herself against a wildly raving Zachary, the only salvation she could think of was to head for the sanctuary of the women's bathroom. Sharon pulled open the main door to the rest room and went inside, believing the sign saying Women would be enough to keep Zachary away. Picking up the tissue paper first in her office was only an afterthought.

She was just opening the white wooden door to the first stall when the main door crashed against the wall behind her, and she whirled around to see Zachary stepping inside. "I don't believe it! Get out of here, you idiot. Can't you read?"

Sharon watched him look around blindly for a moment, taking in the light yellow-painted concrete block walls, the small sink and the row of five white wooden doors that made up the long, narrow room. "The door, St. Clair!" she shouted, exasperated. "Look what it says on the door!"

Zachary turned and looked at the stenciled printing, then turned back to look at Sharon, who had already disappeared behind the door of the first stall. "When are you going to be through in there?" she heard him ask, and she took comfort in his obvious discomfort.

Having installed the new tissue in the chrome holder, Sharon pushed the door open once more, then peeked around it to glare at Zachary. "September!" she replied with a quick dismissive jerk of her head. "Now, go away!"

Letting the first door slam back into place, she then threw back the door to the second stall, entered and heard it slam shut behind her with a satisfying bang. At least he has some gentlemanly good manners left, she soothed herself as she slammed the second roll of tissue paper home before kicking the second door open in order to proceed to the third stall.

But the door stayed open; it didn't swing shut again to soothe her soul with yet another satisfying bang. Jerking her head around as she still held the three rolls of tissue paper close to her body, she saw Zachary's face leering down at her from over the top of the door.

"You had me there for a minute, Shari," she heard him say. "But as we're not open for business, I doubt that it matters that I'm in here."

"It matters to me!" Sharon told him, pulling open the door to the third stall and letting it crash shut behind her. "Can't you take a hint, St. Clair?" she called to him from inside the stall. "I don't want to talk to you. I don't want to look at you. I don't even want to be on the same *planet* with you. And just as soon as I'm finished with this one last job I'm leaving—so that I never, ever have to look at you or listen to you again! Have I made myself perfectly clear?"

"As crystal, Sharon. Tell me, what planet are you aiming for?" she heard Zachary ask, his gibe causing her to growl in exasperation as she ruthlessly jammed the tissue into the holder.

"Ha, ha, very funny. You're a real laugh riot, St. Clair; you ought to be in the movies," Sharon said as her temper got the best of her. "You know very well what I mean. I'm just leaving!"

She waited until she heard the door to the second stall close, then threw open the door to the third stall with all the force she could muster, gaining a large measure of satisfaction from the clunking sound the wood made when it came sharply into contact with Zachary's knees. She didn't make the mistake of standing around in the narrow aisleway to admire her handiwork, but bolted for the fourth stall as fast as she could.

"You know you don't mean that, Shari. Now stop slamming doors and listen to me!" Zachary called after her.

Sharon clapped her hands over her ears and began loudly humming 'The Battle Hymn of the Republic,' trying to block out the sound of his voice.

"You can't leave," Zachary continued to shout. "You love this place. Look, Shari, I've already apologized for getting the wrong impression when I walked in on you and Hugh. I don't know what got into me."

That did it! Sharon had asked him to leave her alone, spelled it out to him in words of one syllable, and still he persisted. Now, she decided with a sharp intake of breath, he was going to get a piece of her mind!

Sharon shot the door open as hard as she could, holding the solid piece of wood ajar to stand as a barrier between Zachary and herself in the narrow aisle. Looking up at him as he hung his head over the top of the door, she sneered, "Nothing 'got into' you, Zachary. You were just being your usual, obnoxious self. Flying off the handle seems to be a hobby of yours. As a matter of fact, the only predictable thing about you is your very *unpredictability*. Is that how you keep your employees on their toes? By being nice one minute and then biting off their heads the next? Well, no thanks. You can just take your kisses and your tantrums somewhere else. *I quit!*"

Her explosion of wrath over, Sharon quickly disappeared behind the last door, but she didn't bother trying to install the one remaining roll of tissue. Her hands were shaking so badly she knew it would be impossible. Instead, she just stood leaning against the side wall a moment, trying to catch her breath as tears pricked behind her tightly shut eyelids.

This wasn't quite the way she had envisioned saying her final goodbye to Wheeler's—playing hide-and-seek in the women's bathroom with an irate soon-to-be ex-boss. She should have just stormed out with Hugh, and then sent someone else to pick up her car later, but her so-called friend had deserted her before she could gather her thoughts enough to do more than hop down from the countertop and make a mad dash for her office.

Now, after counting to ten several times, Sharon leaned her head back against the wall and raised her gaze to the whitewashed ceiling, sniffling self-pityingly a time or two at the curious hand fate had dealt her. "So this is the way the career ends," she mused aloud, "not with a bang but a whimper. The manager of Wheeler's has just resigned in the women's bath-

room. As resignations go, Sharon, old girl, I think this
one lacks something for glamour."

"Are you ready to talk now? Or are you only going
to talk to yourself?"

Zachary's questions jolted Sharon back to reality.
"I'll never be ready to talk to you!" she shouted back
at him. "Not if I live another million years. I've quit.
Resigned. Handed in my notice. I don't have to do
anything I don't want to anymore. Now stand back,
or this door is going to smack you right in the nose."

She counted to three, then slapped her hands against
the door as hard as she could, hoping he hadn't heeded
her warning.

The door didn't budge. She pushed at it again,
leaning all of her weight into the movement. Nothing. The door remained firmly shut, Sharon on one
side, Zachary on the other.

"Let me out of here! You're not playing fair," she
ordered, banging her fists against the door. "Locking
a woman in a bathroom! Who do you think you are?
One of the Marx Brothers? Grow up, St. Clair."

She ground her teeth in impotent fury as she heard
the amusement in Zachary's voice as he answered.
"The Marx Brothers? Oh, I don't know about that.
The way I've been chasing you, I think I feel more like
Mack Sennet doing one of his Keystone Kops chase
scenes. Besides, shame on you, Miss Wheeler. I don't
believe I heard you say 'please.'"

Sharon repeatedly slapped her hands furiously
against her thighs as she looked around the small
booth, considering and then rejecting the ignomi-
nious solution of crawling out of the booth under-

neath the door. "All right," she said at last, forcing an air of politeness into her voice. "Zachary, *please* let me out of here."

Zachary smiled as he heard Sharon's voice and her obvious attempt to control her anger. "No," he replied cheerfully, still standing at his ease, his arms crossed at the elbows, his back leaning comfortably against the stall door. "I don't think so. I'm beginning to think this is the only way I'll be able to make you listen to me. Now, Sharon, are you ready to listen to me?"

"Arrgh!"

Zachary smiled yet again. "I'll take that as a yes. All right, Sharon, here goes. First of all, please accept my apology one more time for reading anything sinister into that little scene with Hugh. I realize now that you were upset and he was merely comforting you. The fact that *I* was the reason you were crying is just one more thing I need to apologize for. I know I wasn't very nice to you yesterday."

"Nice? You were awful!" Sharon's voice was rather thick, as if she were crying yet again. "But you didn't hurt me. I always cry when I get angry, not that it matters anymore. I can take a hint. You don't think I'm a good manager, so just as soon as you let me out of here you'll have my resignation. Unless you want to slip a pen under the door—I can write it on the tissue paper."

Zachary turned his head to look at the door, as if he could see through it to where Sharon stood, probably making a face at him. "Getting a little flippant for a person who's gotten herself locked in a bathroom, aren't you?'' he teased. ''I hate to disappoint you, Sharon, but I *can't* accept your resignation. *Now*, will you listen to me?''

''What do you mean you can't accept my resignation?'' she asked, again pushing on the door. ''You mean you *won't* accept it, don't you? Well, I don't care. And you can't fire me. I've already quit you.''

''You're right there, I can't fire you. I'm not your boss. Oh, I did buy the place from the corporation, but that was only so I could give it away to somebody else last night,'' Zachary informed her evenly, then waited for her reaction.

''Give it away?'' Sharon squeaked. ''But you promised! Who owns us now?''

''Another St. Clair. My father, actually,'' he told her, feeling just as pleased as he had the night before when the idea had first occurred to him. ''As of this morning my father, Lucien St. Clair, owns one hundred percent of Wheeler's Drive-In. You'll love him, and he'll be crazy about the place, just as it is. There's no more St. Clair Theater Corporation to bother you anymore, Shari. My lawyers are already drawing up the necessary papers to transfer ownership.''

At last, his little speech over, although there was still so much he had left unsaid, Zachary moved away from the door, allowing Sharon to exit her temporary prison.

Within seconds he was rewarded with the appearance of her head as she peeked around the corner of the stall, a thoroughly bemused expression on her

beautiful face. Her cornflower-blue eyes were glisten-
ing with unshed tears as she looked up at him, her
dusky pink lips moving as she tried to say something.

"Still going to quit, Shari?" he couldn't resist asking as, slowly, hesitantly, she moved completely into
the narrow aisle that ran in front of the stalls. "My
dad's retired to Florida, so you can't really just leave
the place to run itself, can you? I'm still going to ad-
vance the money for all the necessary repairs. I mean,
Gertrude's nice and all that, but I don't think we
should go on encouraging her to wander. Come on,
honey, what do you say? Will you stay now?"

"What do I say?" Sharon told him slowly, her voice
husky with passion, "I'll tell you what I say. I say that
you are...the most hateful...thoroughly despicable...underhanded...*conniving* man who has ever
lived!"

Zachary stepped back against the wall, involuntarily clutching the roll of bathroom tissue Sharon
jabbed sharply into his midsection as she swept past
him at top speed and ran out into the sunlight.

"Women!" he shouted into the empty room, his
angry condemnation echoing back at him from the
concrete block walls as he ran after Sharon. But she
had already reached her car and was in the process of
backing out of the parking area. "Sharon!" he yelled
over the sound of the engine, banging his hands
against the hood of the station wagon, "Wait!"

She either didn't hear him or refused to acknowledge him, and a moment later the only sounds left in
the parking area were the fiercely soft whisperings of

Zachary St. Clair as he cursed himself for being the biggest fool of all time.

The crickets are sure in full voice tonight, Sharon thought idly as she sat slumped in her cotton night-gown on one side of the old wooden porch swing, absently pushing it back and forth with the force of the foot she had propped against the nearby porch railing.

I can almost hear a couple of them furiously rubbing their little legs together, chirping out the message far and wide to all their friends, she mused, saying aloud: "Sharon Wheeler's made a fool of herself; Sharon Wheeler's made a fool of herself."

It was past midnight, fully twelve hours since Zachary had stormed into the snack bar to set off the bizarre chain of events that had sent Sharon scurrying for the shelter of her bedroom, where she had hidden herself away until an hour ago, like some wanted criminal on the lam from the law.

Hunger had finally prodded her out of her seclusion, and she had just finished downing half a cold chicken, a heaping mound of day-old potato salad and a gargantuan slice of homemade double chocolate layer cake. "I feel sick," she told the chorus of insects, although she knew that her recent meal had little to do with the queasy feeling in her stomach.

"Oh, Popsie, what do I do now?" she wailed aloud, rising from the swing to stand at the railing, looking out over the large front yard that surrounded the isolated century-old farmhouse her grandfather had left to her directly, circumventing her father's decision to sell everything that wasn't nailed down just as soon as Al Wheeler's will was read so that he and his young second wife could move to California.

"The drive-in has been sold again, Popsie," Sharon said, turning back toward the swing and talking as if her grandfather was once again sitting in his favorite spot, his unlit pipe stuck firmly between his gleaming, store-bought teeth. "It's privately owned again, but the new owner lives in Florida. I'm supposed to stay on as manager, but I don't know if I can. You see, there's something about the whole thing that I don't think I can live with."

Sharon closed her eyes, and then rubbed one hand against her mouth, trying to find some way to tell her grandfather about Zachary St. Clair. How could she tell her grandfather, even his spirit, that she believed Zachary had only sold Wheeler's in some perverted act of charity?

"I get the idea he's just cast himself in the role of Daddy Warbucks," she said, feeling like some storm-tossed orphan who'd just been handed a lollipop.

That was the only explanation she could think of for Zachary to have done what he had. It certainly wasn't a good move for him to have made economically, and Zachary had already proved to her that he was first and foremost a businessman. Well, if he wanted to play philanthropist, *she* wasn't going to stay around to applaud.

That was the reason she had stormed out of the drive-in, barely able to see past the red-hot fury that burned in her eyes, that pulsated throughout her entire disillusioned body.

She hadn't believed she had been flattering herself with what she had thought earlier, what she was still thinking. Zachary had made it all too clear that he found her attractive, even desirable. After all, his kisses haven't been exactly platonic!

Heaven only knows, I was so dazzled by his unexpected gentleness, so intrigued by his many moods, so wildly attracted to him physically, that he could have had me for the taking, she thought now, feeling her cheeks grow hot with shame as she remembered their rather torrid interlude the day before in the front seat of his sports car.

"Talk about your infatuations. Lord, was I naïve. I actually thought he cared for me. Well, so much for foolish dreams. I should have known better. Anyone would think I actually believe that stuff Hollywood is always putting on the screen.

"Now, just when I think he's beginning to care for me, he signs me up for the part of Orphan Annie. Well, Zachary St. Clair has another thought coming. Sharon Wheeler is nobody's charity case!" she declared feelingly, lifting her chin proudly.

She was silent for a few moments, waiting for the rush of satisfaction that she should have been feeling at this pronouncement of her overwhelming integrity, but it didn't come.

"Well, anyway," she tried to defend herself, fidgeting a bit as she began to feel uncomfortable in her cloak of righteousness, "I have the satisfaction of knowing that I was right to tell him how despicable I think he is. After all, did he think I just came down in the last rain, as Popsie used to say, to fall for some story that he was acting out of concern for his stock-holders? If he wants to ease his conscience, he can find another place to toss his money.''

He could have been trying to be your friend, her inner self told her, offering one solution.

"Hah! That would be the day," she answered, scoffing at such foolishness. "I can see us now, ex-changing friendly Christmas cards every year. 'All the best of the season; let's do lunch.' Not on your life! Zachary doesn't know the meaning of the word friend. Maybe I was wrong about the charity; maybe he's trying to *buy* me!''

All right, her inner voice countered, still trying to reason with her, *forget the friendship bit. But how do you explain away involving his own father in the deal? Do you really think Lucien St. Clair would allow himself to be a party to any hanky-panky going on between his son and his theater manager?*

"He's Zachary's father, isn't he?" Sharon pointed out meanly. "He probably taught his son everything he knows. Like father, like son, they always say."

Oh, you're something else, aren't you, Sharon Wheeler, her conscience interrupted. *What's the mat-ter? Is your nose out of joint because he didn't drop to his knees and declare his undying love for you? Be-cause he didn't tell you that he was giving the drive-in away so that he could remove any obstacles that could stand between you and his love for you? I suppose you wanted a formal proposal of marriage, too—just be-cause he kissed you? My gracious, I can almost hear a violin playing in the background. You don't want much, do you, Sharon Joan Wheeler? Only the whole*

*world, all neatly tied up in a pretty package, and with
a big red ribbon on top.*

Sharon clapped her hands over her ears, trying hard
to drown out her silent accuser. She turned back to
look warily at the swing, convinced that somehow her
Popsie had to be there—talking to her in that way he'd
always had of cutting through all her nonsense and
getting straight to the heart of things.

"All right, all right!" she cried, surrendering at last
to the truth. "I don't hate Zachary for giving his father the drive-in. I know he never wanted the theater
in the first place—hated the very fact that it was a part
of his so-modern theater circuit—but I can't shake the
feeling that he also did it out of some misdirected
expression of charity. But even if I don't know exactly *why* he did it, I'm being an ungrateful idiot to
even *care* why he did it. I should be doing handstands
that he *did* do it! I must be crazy, looking a gift horse
in the mouth. With the owner in Florida, and Zachary's promise to make the repairs, it's almost like I have
Wheeler's back as my very own. I should be the hap-
piest woman in the world!"

So, what's the problem? the nagging voice asked.

Sharon sat down on the swing once more, tucking
her legs up under her chin and wrapping her arms
around her knees. Her voice cracked a bit as she rested
her chin on her knees and whispered, "Oh, Popsie,
you know what's wrong. I've only known the man for
less than a week, but I know what's wrong with me.
It's knowing that he did it only because he feels sorry

for me, not because he loves me. It's knowing that if Zachary doesn't love me, nothing—not even having the drive-in back—will ever be able to make me feel happy ever again."

Chapter Eight

It had been two days since Sharon had stormed out of the women's bathroom at Wheeler's Drive-In and driven out of Zachary's life. Two days, six hours and seventeen minutes, he corrected mentally, peering at his watch as he sat at the far end of the bar in his hotel, slowly nursing a second, unsatisfying Scotch.

Stanley Wojewodzki stood halfway down the length of the bar, drying shot glasses with a towel, having tried without success to draw Zachary into a conversation concerning the total inability of the Philadelphia Phillies to come up with a good left-handed pitcher to replace Steve Carleton.

Zachary felt rather guilty at his own impoliteness, but he couldn't find it within himself to concentrate on anything more morally uplifting than his intention to get himself completely and numbly drunk in the shortest possible time. As he had never been much of a drinker, he was still sober—and developing a healthy dislike for Scotch.

You really blew it this time, St. Clair, a small inner voice needled him as he threw back the last of his drink with a grimace of distaste and held out his glass to signal Stosh for a refill. Obviously his brain was still functioning, and he needed another dose of liquid amnesia.

I thought you were supposed to be the silver-tongued wheeler-dealer, the great negotiator, the man who could sell ice to the Eskimos. Some salesman. Not only wouldn't Sharon buy what you were selling—you couldn't even give it away.

His timing was off, that's all, he argued silently, putting another twenty dollar bill on the bar. He should have waited until Sharon had cooled down after his stupid reaction to seeing Hugh Kingsley hovering over her like some fairy godmother about to wave a wand and make it all better. But he was afraid she'd run away before he could explain what he'd done, and he wouldn't be able to find her.

Sure, you were only thinking of her. What a guy. Isn't there a Nobel prize for people as pure of heart as you? In a pig's eye, you were thinking of her. What you were doing, St. Clair, was showing off for the lady. You were so full of your own brilliance that you couldn't wait to share it with her, dazzle her a bit. Nice play, Shakespeare. What do you have in mind for an encore?

Zachary squirmed a bit on the bar stool, unable to answer his own question. He knew where to find her. He'd known since speaking with George Blakeman

yesterday, after it became obvious to him that Sharon
wasn't about to show up at Wheeler's. And no matter
how much soul-searching he did, no matter how hard
he had tried to rationalize it away, he knew there was
only one reason he hadn't driven out to Sharon's
country home to plead his case.

He was afraid.

*All right! Now you're talking. Let's brainstorm this
for a minute, run this concept up the old flagpole and
see if anybody salutes! The great Zachary is afraid.
Why?*

God, Zachary thought, wincing, even his subcon-
scious was beginning to sound like the corporate ri-
diculousness he'd been living with for so long—for too
long, if he could still be considered any judge in the
matter.

Hey, don't blame me, his inner self protested.
*Where do you think I got this stuff—some mail order
catalog? Now stop stonewalling and start giving with
some answers. Why are you so afraid of a small
blonde only half your weight?*

Because he cared about her! he admitted. Because
she was hurting, and he was to blame—even if he
didn't know how. He, with his grand schemes and his
funny little games. Even when he tried to help her, he
hurt her, and the last thing he wanted to do now was
hurt her again. *I don't know what to do, which way to
jump. I've never felt so stupid or so useless in my life.*

"Zachary? What in blue blazes are you doing in
here? I asked at the desk and some handsome-looking
fella with real white teeth said I'd find you here. You

know him? Since when do you start drinking before dinner?''

Zachary's spine stiffened and he lifted his head slowly to look into the mirror behind the back bar. "Hello, Dad," he said at last, wondering wildly just when the Fates would think he'd had enough and back off for a while. "I already ate. We dine early in Pennsylvania. What brings you up here? Did Mother throw you out?''

Lucien St. Clair chuckled softly and then lowered his long frame onto the next bar stool. "Your mother's off to the Bahamas with some friends from the club. Something to do with good prices on jewelry, I believe. So, what's this about giving me a theater as a present? Your mother isn't exactly known for keeping telephone messages straight, you know, especially when she's on the scent of a bargain. Why on earth would you want to give me a theater? The corporation owns hundreds.''

Shaking his head ruefully, Zachary summoned up a weak smile. "Not like this one, Dad. Not like this one. Wheeler's Drive-In just happens to be the oldest operating drive-in movie in America. And don't be too thrilled. It's going to cost us a bundle just to get the place back on its feet.''

"A drive-in? You've got to be kidding! Where is it? Texas? How many screens?''

Zachary lowered his head once more, rubbing the side of his neck as he muttered, "Five miles from here. One screen. A carbon house with two ancient projectors. Gloria Swanson and Veronica Lake. And, oh, yes—sauerkraut.''

Lucien reached over and removed the glass that was sitting in front of his son, carefully smelling the liquid inside. "Nope, it's just Scotch. I thought maybe you were drinking something weird. Now, you want to run that one by me again, son? I can't believe I heard you right the first time."

"How may I serve you, sir?" Stosh asked, walking up to the end of the bar. "Hey! You two related? You sure do look alike. You drink Scotch, too? Maybe you're a beer man. We got your domestic, your imported, your light, your—"

"Stosh!" Zachary said, smiling in a way that caused his father to look at him closely. "You're just the man I need. I have to go up to my room and make a phone call. Maybe you can fill my father in about Wheeler's Drive-In. He's the new owner."

"You bought Wheeler's?" the bartender asked, a wide grin splitting his chubby face. "How about that! Well, you came to the right place if you want to hear all about Wheeler's. Me and the wife met there, you know. I told your son all about it the other night. Let's see, where do I start? Well, first, you got your double features, of course, and your cartoons. You also got your snack bar, now that's really something—"

"Zachary," Lucien called weakly after his son, who was already halfway out of the bar. "You wouldn't leave me here like this, would you?"

"I'll be right back, Dad," he said, not turning around or else his father would see the amused look on his face. "Stosh will entertain you while I'm gone."

The older St. Clair watched his son leave, then turned back to listen to the bartender, a painfully polite expression on his face.

"That was Zachary on the phone, Shari," George Blakeman said, easing himself into his favorite chair in the living room of his small house. "He wanted to know if I'd heard from you. He said he called your house but there was no answer. He sounded upset."

Sharon hopped up from the comfortable, worn couch she was lying on and looked quickly around the room, as if seeking the nearest exit. "You didn't tell him I was here, did you, George? You know I don't want to see him again—ever."

"Relax, I didn't tell him. But you're going to have to see him sometime, aren't you? After all, you're working for his father now. Right?"

Sharon flopped back down onto the couch, resting her elbows on her knees. "I don't think so, George. That's really what I came here to talk about, although I guess I've been too busy bending your ear about my miserable love life to get around to the subject. I haven't agreed to manage the place yet, and I'm not sure I want to."

"How can you *not* agree when you know that if you don't you'll have lost any chance you ever had of keeping a Wheeler as part of the place? You love that drive-in. You lasted through two other owners. Right? Do you think Al would want you to abandon it now—just to soothe your injured pride?"

Sharon sank back against the soft cushions, sighing. "You aren't playing fair. Popsie wouldn't want

me to accept charity, just so I could stay a part of
Wheeler's.''

George got up from his chair and walked to the
television set, turning down the sound. Zachary's
phone call had interrupted the rerun they had been
watching, and he no longer knew which of the actors
with day-old beards were the cops and which were the
bad guys. "Shari, I think you've been watching too
many movies. He was just making an honest gesture
of friendship, hunting for a way to keep the place open
and still keep his stockholders happy. I think he likes
the drive-in in spite of himself. The guy couldn't have
been nicer to me, and after I'd taken a swing at him,
too. You ought to talk to him, give him a chance to
explain. Right?''

"You men!" Sharon exclaimed incredulously.
"When you get right down to it, you all stick together. People don't buy businesses just to give them
away, for heaven's sake. Not without a good reason,
anyway. Charity's fine, huh? Sure, let's toss poor
Shari a bone!''

"Maybe he had a good reason for being nice to
you," George suggested. "From what you told me
tonight at the dinner table, the two of you were getting pretty chummy there for a while. Right?''

Sharon made a face at her old friend. "Forget I ever
brought up the idea. It was just a few kisses, George,
not a scene from *A Man and a Woman*. But if his
'friendly gesture' wasn't charity, why hasn't he come
to see me to explain? It's been two days.''

George laughed, shaking his head. "Are you the
same Sharon Wheeler who almost ran out of here a

minute ago because you thought I might have told Zachary that you were here? No wonder the man sounded so upset. If you've been acting as hot and cold around him he'll be lucky if he knows which way to jump. Right?''

Sharon's mind went unbidden to her actions of the previous few days, her belligerence that had turned to passion, then anger. And she had accused Zachary of being mercurial! She should be ashamed of herself. ''I don't care to think about my experiences with Mr. St. Clair, if you please,'' she informed George firmly, tilting her chin in defiance.

''All right. Then think about this a moment, Shari. You have to come to some sort of a decision soon. We've had a break, since we're only open three nights this week, but the film's due in tomorrow morning, and somebody has to get the show made up for tomorrow night. Right? And don't ask me to do it. I'm on vacation.''

Sharon bit on the side of her thumb as she considered what to do next. She'd hidden out in her house, working on a project connected with her part-time job until George had called that afternoon, wanting to know why Zachary St. Clair was looking for her, and she'd spent the hours since then alternately crying out her troubles to her old friend and finding excuses for not going back to her empty, silent house.

She was so confused. Didn't she have enough to think about, trying to convince herself that Zachary meant nothing, even less than nothing, to her? Did she have to worry about Wheeler's, too? After all, it wasn't like it was really hers. Oh, she might have continued to think of it as hers, even after the theater had been sold and then sold again, but somehow the atmosphere had changed once Zachary had come on the scene.

She was beginning to see his point about Wheeler's. The drive-in wasn't exactly a money-maker, not in the sense that the multiscreen houses in the area were. It had been fine for her grandfather, who had an independent income to fall back on, but nobody was ever going to get rich running a theater that could only remain open from late May until October. Even she, Sharon, had to take on extra jobs to make ends meet. An owner like Zachary's father, retired and self-sufficient, was the perfect answer, much as she hated to admit it.

As if he could read her mind, George said now, "Al knew the drive-in couldn't stand on its own, Shari. If you think about it, we make most of our money at the snack bar. Right?"

"I guess so," Sharon mumbled, listening to these damning words in spite of herself.

"That's why he didn't leave it to you in his will," her old friend pushed on. "I think he was hoping you'd see it as a chance to strike out on your own once he was gone, build a life for yourself separate from Wheeler's. Lord only knew Al wasn't counting on his son to hold on to it. Jim never liked the place. Right?"

Sharon reached into the pocket of her shorts for a tissue, which she then blotted against the tears on her cheeks. "You waited six years to tell me all this, George? And I guess you only stayed on because of me. Now I really feel awful. I thought I was a businesswoman, but I've only been a little girl playing house. Only instead of playing with dolls and having tea parties, I've been showing movies and pushing popcorn. Oh, George, I feel like such a fool!''

The old man turned his head away, seemingly to avoid looking directly at Sharon. ''Yeah, well, there's no fool like an old fool, because I went right on playing the game with you, even though I knew better. Up until a few minutes ago I was still so caught up in the game I was trying to get you to accept St. Clair's offer and pretending your grandfather would have wanted you to stay. But no more. It's time we all stopped playing make-believe.''

''So what do I do now? I've already talked you into hiding me here tonight, but I can't keep avoiding Zachary forever.''

''Yes. It looks like you've got a decision to make. Right?''

Sharon's mind immediately conjured up a picture of Zachary and she sniffed a time or two, then slipped the tissue back into her pocket. But she knew George wasn't thinking about her supposed love life. ''You mean about Wheeler's, don't you? But there's really no decision to make. Zachary's father owns it; it's up to him to say who runs the place for him. Maybe he'll even want to manage it himself.''

''That's what the place needs, all right. Another old man trying to recreate the past,'' George slid in quietly. ''And who do you think is going to run Gloria and Veronica? None of those young puppies who work in the platter houses know the first thing about real projectors. Right?''

"Wouldn't you—"

"Not in a million years. I learned my lesson Sunday night. I can't take the pressure anymore. If you go, I go."

Sharon sat up very straight. "Well *somebody* has to run the projectors tomorrow. The ads are already on the paper for this weekend's show. Maybe Zachary—oh, who do I think I'm kidding—Zachary St. Clair wouldn't know a projector head from Mr. Potato Head. He's a businessman, not a projectionist. What will he do?"

George walked over and turned up the sound on the television. "I don't know. And why do you care what he does? You don't even like the guy. Right? Or do you still have some more decisions to make?"

"No, George," she said firmly. "My decisions are all made. I'm going to leave Wheeler's *and* the St. Clairs to fend for themselves. From now on, they can just count me out!"

Friday morning came and made liars of them all.

George was up and out early, leaving a note on the kitchen table telling Sharon he was taking his car to the garage to have the tires rotated.

Sharon didn't eat the breakfast George had left warming in the oven for her, using the back of his note to scribble a message thanking him for his hospitality and saying that she had just remembered she had promised to feed a vacationing friend's cat.

Lucien had left a note at the hotel desk, telling Zachary he had chipped a tooth at breakfast and had gone off to see a local dentist.

Zachary, who had no one else left to lie to, got into his sports car after reading his father's message and lied to himself, thinking he was merely going for a mind-clearing ride in the country.

And at twenty minutes past nine that Friday morning, the first meeting of the unofficial Liar's Club was called to order in the snack bar of Wheeler's Drive-In.

"Stosh!" Zachary said as he walked into the snack bar. "What are you doing here?"

The bartender, smiling as he stood just behind the Formica bar, clad in red-and-white-striped Bermuda shorts and a bright red cotton knit shirt, replied happily, "It's my day off, and Lucien asked me to drive him out here and sort of show him around the place. I've never seen it from this side before. Look at this. You got your hot butter holder, your steamer table, your popcorn popper. Did you ever see such a big can of jalapeño peppers?"

"Where's my dad now?" Zachary could hear voices coming from the projection booth, and he was wondering who was in there with his father. "How did you get through the gate?"

Stosh explained that they had been having a bit of a problem there, standing outside the gate trying to figure out what to do next, but then this old guy in a battered Plymouth had driven up and let them in with his key. Lucien and the old guy had been walking around the grounds, but now they were inside, looking at some funny-looking machines in the other room.

An old guy in a battered Plymouth? "George? George is here? I don't know how I missed seeing his car," Zachary commented as he bent down to work his way under the counter. "Is there a pretty blonde with him?"

"Now, would I be in here looking at a popcorn machine if there was a pretty blonde around?" Stosh asked, throwing Zachary a broad wink. "Oh, ho. Don't look now, but I think one just walked in."

Zachary swiveled around quickly, in time to see Sharon standing just inside the door, looking like one of the Christians about to say hello to the lions. "Sharon!" he called, just as she seemed ready to bolt. "Thank God you're here. I have to talk to you."

"I came to make up tonight's film, if it's arrived," she told him, her head high as she walked toward the Formica bar. "I see George is already here, so I'll assume that all I'll have to do is prepare the beef barbecue for the weekend and check on our kitchen supplies."

Zachary backed up a few paces as she joined him inside the enclosed snack bar serving area, not wanting to make her feel as if he was crowding her. "I don't know if George is working or not. My father just came in unexpectedly from Florida to inspect the place. I believe they're together now, in the projection booth. I'd like you to meet my dad, if you want to."

Sharon answered without really looking at him. "If I'm going to be working for the gentleman," she said, repositioning a salt shaker one-half inch closer to the napkin holder, "I imagine I should take the time to meet him. Your presence, however, I believe to be entirely superfluous. Now, if you'll excuse me?''

Zachary automatically stepped to one side to let Sharon pass by, wondering what it was about the look in her big blue eyes that made him feel as if he had been guilty of kicking a helpless puppy. "I'll go with you anyway," he called after her. "Sometimes my father takes a bit of explaining."

As soon as he rounded the corner and entered the projection room, Zachary knew he had been right. His father hadn't been in town a full day and already he was up to his old tricks.

"And I tell you it was Joan Crawford," he heard his father arguing with George, who was standing beside the worktable examining a reel of film and looking like a man about to commit mayhem.

"Bette Davis, and I've got five dollars here that says I'm right," George declared, digging in his pocket for the money. "Ah, here's Sharon, the girl I was telling you about, Lucien. She'll know. She has all that stuff tucked up in her pretty little head."

"What's the problem, George?" Sharon asked just as Zachary came up behind her, silently making a face at his father that literally begged the older man to be good. "Are you two having a disagreement?"

"Lucien here says it was Joan Crawford who made a cameo appearance in *Scent of Mystery*, and we all know it was Bette Davis. Right? Tell him, Shari."

"Well, George," Sharon began hesitantly, "to tell you the truth, I don't really think I know—"

"You're both wrong. It was Elizabeth Taylor," Zachary said quickly, stepping around Sharon to approach his father. "How's the tooth, Dad? You don't look any the worse for wear."

"So I lied," Lucien retorted, unrepentant, motioning with his head toward Sharon. "Who's this? My manager? George said she was pretty, but now I know why you were trying to drown yourself in that bar. George told me all about it. You really made a botch of things. I must say I expected a little more finesse from you. What's the matter, son, losing your touch?"

"*Oh!* I was right all along. You're all alike!" Sharon yelled at the three men, turning to leave. "I don't know why I came here in the first place. I must have been out of my mind, feeling sorry for all of you. Well, you can just forget it. I'm leaving. Make your own damn barbecue!"

Sharon ran back into the snack bar, past the man in the awful Bermuda shorts, and out into the sunlight. She didn't make the mistake of heading for the women's bathroom again, but instead made for the ticket booth, thinking to lock herself inside until Zachary gave up and went away.

As she ran she tried to understand what had prompted her to say she wanted to meet her new boss. She had only come to the drive-in to help out temporarily, until someone could be brought in to take her place; she certainly had no intention of staying on as manager.

But when she had opened her mouth to tell Zachary that, something entirely different had come out, and now she had given him the impression that she had accepted the job. "No wonder they say blondes are dumb!'' she muttered as she jogged along, knowing full well that Zachary was only one row behind her and coming up fast.

Changing direction, she headed for the playground, and hopped onto the merry-go-round, pushing with one foot to set the circular metal disk in motion. She was being ridiculous, juvenile, but all she wanted to do was spin round and round, as her jumbled thoughts were doing, hoping against hope that she would somehow be granted time to figure out what to do next.

She had spun around five or six times, not quite long enough to get dizzy, when suddenly she felt her upper body being surrounded by two strong masculine arms, and she had no choice but to allow herself to be lifted back onto solid ground.

Her eyes tightly closed, she leaned back weakly against Zachary, taking in the solidness of his body, the spicy scent of his after shave, the heat of his embrace, and she knew her sudden giddiness was not a result of either her flight from the projection booth or her short ride on the merry-go-round.

She was dizzy from his nearness, breathless with anticipation as to what he would do next. Would he kiss her? He was holding her in a way that told her she could run again if she chose, and this time, perhaps, he wouldn't follow. He was giving her a choice.

And the last thing she wanted at that moment was a choice. She wanted him to take charge, to demand that she surrender to his kiss, to his embrace, to his every desire. He had already stepped into her life and turned it upside down; why couldn't he continue to dictate to her? Then she could tell herself that she had nothing to do with the decision. That he had coerced her, dazzled her with gifts, seduced her with his commanding physical attraction.

But no, he just continued to hold her against him, his arms loosely draped around her waist, his cheek pressed against her hair. He didn't say anything, explain anything, ask anything—take anything. He just gave her time, all the time she didn't want to take, to make the next move.

She wanted to turn in his arms and be held the way a woman wants to be held, kissed the way a woman longs to be kissed. But would he think she was kissing him out of love for him—or because he had made some absurd humanitarian gesture and saved Wheeler's?

Why, oh why, had she made that stupid crack back at the snackbar? Why had she run away—again? Why hadn't she told him immediately that she didn't want to stay at Wheeler's as if both she and it were some sort of charity cases he had contributed to, told him that she loved him for himself, and then stood back to wait for his next move.

Because then there might not have been a next move, her inner voice pointed out prudently. *Because, if you'd told him you love him he might have turned on his heel and beaten a path back to New York so fast you'd have been blown down in the breeze. Because even if you might think he wants you, in today's world wanting a person and loving her are two very separate things.*

"Sharon? Have I knocked the wind out of you? You've been standing here for two minutes and you haven't either yelled at me, kicked me in the shins or tried to run away. Does this mean you're ready to talk?"

I love his voice, Sharon thought randomly, tilting her head slightly to one side as his husky tones, spoken so close beside her ear, sent a shiver down the side of her neck. "Talk?" she repeated, fumbling for something to say. "What do you want to talk about? Your father seems very like you, and he and George seem to be hitting it off nicely. Actually, they looked like two little boys set loose in a candy store, the way they were working together making up tonight's feature."

"Bully for good old George and good old Lucien," Zachary told her, slowly turning her around to face him. "I couldn't be happier for them. No, Shari. I don't want to talk about my father and George."

Sharon moistened her suddenly dry lips. "Then I guess you must be wondering about my, er, rather dramatic reaction the other day to your decision to give the drive-in to your father." She purposely looked down at her toes as she gave a forced laugh and said, "I imagine you must have figured out by now that I thought you had done it as a form of charity. Silly, aren't I?"

"Not so silly, Sharon. That same thought occurred to me as I stood there trying to catch my breath after you jammed that roll of bathroom tissue into my gut like a football," Zachary answered, running his hands up and down her bare upper arms. "I wish you had given me a chance to explain instead of running off like that.''

''Well, it took me a little time, but I did realize that you hadn't meant anything like that. You didn't, did you?'' she asked, looking up at him a moment, then quickly averting her eyes when she saw the passionate expression in his.

''No, Sharon, it wasn't charity,'' she heard him answer, and breathed a sigh of relief. ''The drive-in was standing between us, and I wanted it out of the way. You see, no matter how good my intentions, the more I looked at Wheeler's, the more I knew it could never fit into the St. Clair Theater Corporation. It just isn't our sort of house. There's no way I could have justified the money it would take to update this place.''

''Update it? You mean put in platters. Replace Gloria and Veronica?''

''Don't bite my head off,'' he told her. ''I said I couldn't do it, didn't I? But if I'd shut it down, you'd never have spoken to me again. For some strange reason, that bothered me. It bothered me a lot.''

Sharon bit her lip to hide a smile. ''It did?''

''Yes, it did. But don't get a big head, lady, because I didn't buy it just so we could stop fighting over it.''

''No, you didn't, did you? You didn't even keep it for yourself,'' Sharon interrupted, seeing the faraway expression in Zachary's eyes. ''You gave it to your father.''

''In lieu of an apology, yes, I did,'' he told her, taking her hand and starting the walk back to the projection booth. ''Dad loves places like this, small one-owner theaters. After I'd finally gotten him to let me update and expand our operations, the heart seemed to go out of him, only I was too blind to see it. When the company went public a few years ago, Dad retired. I think he's been miserable, but too proud of me to complain. Wheeler's is perfect for him. He and Mother can have their winters in Florida, and they can come up here in the summer and be theater operators again."

You seem to have everything all tied up in a nice little bow, Sharon thought as they walked along. *But, if Lucien is going to run the place, where do I come in? Even more to the point—do I want to come in? Do I still want to be a part of Wheeler's? Last night I didn't think so. But now?*

"It sounds nice, Zachary," she said aloud, hoping he couldn't hear the unhappiness in her voice. Her emotions were swinging back and forth so rapidly that she couldn't figure out if she was happy for him, sad for herself or just plain confused. "Maybe Lucien will want George to stick around, as sort of an assistant projectionist?"

Zachary nodded. "I think so. And you can go back to pushing your hot dogs with sauerkraut. I saw the books, Shari, and I know the snack bar is where most of the profits come from. It seems like a good arrangement all round, and the stockholders can't say anything because I made them a ten percent profit on the sale. Now, are you still angry with me?"

"Angry with you?" Sharon repeated dully, feeling like a disillusioned child who had yearned for the moon only to learn that it was out of reach. Then she

forced a lighter tone into her voice. "Of course I'm
not. I'm flattered that you would think enough of me
to handpick my next boss. I love this place, you know.
I even love it enough to have finally given in and
agreed to go on working for you if you hadn't sold it."

Zachary stopped walking and turned her around to
face him once more. "But then I couldn't know that,
could I, especially when we haven't been able to discuss the place without clawing at each other like cats.
But I was still taking a chance, wasn't I? You might
even have decided that you hated me enough to want
nothing more to do with *any* St. Clair."

"And that bothered you." Sharon's heart began to
beat a little faster. "That I might not want to have
anything to do with you—I mean, with a St. Clair."

Zachary drew her against his chest and lifted her
chin with his finger. "Again, Shari, don't go getting
power mad. After all, it might just be that I don't like
to lose." His head began to slowly move down toward hers as she instinctively withdrew at his words.
"But then again, I might have another reason entirely."

Sharon was lost, and she knew it. She surrendered
to his kiss, trying wordlessly to communicate all that
she felt with her mouth, her hands, her body. His response was immediate, and very rewarding.

But it wasn't the answer she was looking for, it was
only another question.

Chapter Nine

The remainder of the day went smoothly, Sharon and Zachary having privately assured themselves that if everything between them wasn't perfect, it was at least considerably better than it had been twenty-four hours earlier. For the time being, that had to be enough.

They spent the rest of the afternoon working side by side in the snack bar, with Sharon giving the orders and Zachary docilely carrying them out.

George and Lucien remained closeted together in the projection booth, checking the newly arrived release prints of that weekend's feature presentations by hand before placing each of the reels in its own separate numbered storage bin, while comparing notes on their combined almost-century-long careers in the theater business.

Stosh, who had passed the hours wandering back and forth between the snack bar and the projection booth, showed no signs of becoming bored, and Sharon finally set him to work popping popcorn, a job the bartender accepted as a high honor indeed.

The five met in the snack bar for a quick meal of Wheeler's special steak sandwiches before the rest of the crew showed up, and it was only after Sharon had set the teenage girls to work that Lucien and George made their little announcement.

They were going back to George's house to look at his old scrapbooks.

"But I thought you were going to run the movies?" Sharon asked in confusion, looking at her old friend.

"George explained that Zachary had given him the week off, Sharon," Lucien supplied as George abruptly developed an overwhelming interest in the ice cream sandwich he was eating. "It doesn't seem fair to cut his vacation short, does it, considering the fact that we have two other licensed projectionists on the grounds?"

Sharon looked around the small circle for a moment, her bewildered gaze finally focusing on Zachary, who was leaning against the counter next to the hot dog carousel, a devilish grin on his face. "Him?" she asked incredulously. "You've got to be joking."

Zachary straightened, looking assessingly at his father. The man had a smile that reminded him that Lucien never had much of a head for subtlety. Obviously George and Lucien had spent the afternoon talking about more than their glorious pasts. *Methinks I smell the scent of matchmaking in the air,* he thought in wry amusement, inclining his head to the man in acknowledgment of his intentions.

Then he looked over at Sharon, who was showing all the outward signs of panic. *There's another one who should never play poker,* his meaner self decided. *Hugh Kingsley must be one heck of a rotten gin rummy player if he can't read Sharon like a book. She'd rather face a horde of stampeding buffalo than work with me in that projection booth. I wonder why.*

"You're right, Dad," he said at last. "I did give George the week off. But it shouldn't take two people to run the projectors. I'll do it alone. That way Sharon can stay in here where she belongs—out of trouble."

"Now just a darn minute!" Sharon exclaimed hotly, falling right into his trap just as Zachary knew she would. "George! Are you really going to let him in there alone with Veronica and Gloria?"

"Doesn't bother me any," George said, shrugging. "Lucien here says Zachary can do it. He's the boss, Shari. Right?"

"And what does that make me—chopped liver?" she countered, busily untying her apron and slamming it down on the counter. "I'm still the manager here if I remember correctly. Stay out here where I *belong*, will I? Well, we'll see about that! Come on, St. Clair, why don't you show me what you can do."

"Yes, boss," Zachary answered with dutiful subservience, stepping forward quickly to hold open the door to the projection booth and allow Sharon to enter ahead of him. He hesitated a moment, then looked back to see his father and George shaking hands as if congratulating each other. "You're quite a pair of connivers, you know that? Well, don't be surprised if your Machiavellian scheme backfires and the lady murders me before the cartoon is over."

"If she does, son, I wash my hands of you," Zachary heard Lucien say just before the sound of cabinet doors being slammed inside the projection booth commanded his attention and he stepped inside the room, closing the door behind him.

He saw Sharon over at the worktable, ruthlessly rooting through a cardboard box she had unearthed from somewhere in the room. "What are you looking for?" he asked, walking up behind her.

Sharon turned abruptly, nearly colliding with him, a small can in one hand, a paintbrush in the other. "You should know," she told him, ducking around him and moving to the center of the room. "After all, you were the one who said we'd always be fighting if we had to deal together in business. Getting the snack bar organized is one thing, but I don't think our relationship—if you want to call what we have a relationship—could stand actually working together in here for a full weekend without this."

Zachary reached up a hand to scratch his head, realizing that she was holding an open can of yellow paint. "I call it a relationship, Shari," he said softly, comprehension slowly dawning on him. "But you're not really serious about this, are you? I mean, I can remember Charlie Barrows telling me about old-time projectionists doing this when they couldn't get along together, but I can't believe—"

"Believe it," Sharon told him, striding over to the front of the projection booth between the two projectors and then dropping to her knees. "I'm painting a line down the middle of the room. You stay on your side, and I'll stay on mine. It's the only way we're going to be able to make this thing work. Now, who do you want, Gloria or Veronica?"

Zachary leaned back against the worktable and watched as Sharon began painting a five-inch-wide yellow line on the floor down the middle of the booth. "The door to the snack bar is on Veronica's side. I'll take her," he said, deliberately trying to upset her.

"Figures," he heard her mutter, and then he lost interest in the topic and just enjoyed the spectacle of watching Sharon backing her way across the booth on her knees, the yellow line growing longer as she went.

"You do nice work," he said when she had finished. "You never told me what you do in the off-season. Perhaps you hire yourself out as a house-painter."

"Wrong. I teach martial arts at a girls' school, so they can learn to defend themselves against men with a perverted sense of humor," she said as she tapped the lid back on the can and returned it to the cabinet.

"No, you don't," Zachary responded, carefully stepping over the wet paint to his side of the room. "If you did you wouldn't have had to paint that line. You could have just . . . *tossed* me for which projector you wanted. Besides, I'm being serious, Sharon. I realized the other day that I know very little about you. What *do* you do in the off-season? Remember, I saw your salary listed in the books. You must do something else besides managing the theater.''

Zachary surprised himself with the depth of his interest, knowing that in the past he hadn't cared if the women he knew wrapped themselves in plastic sheeting and hung themselves in the closet between dates with him. Sharon intrigued him, and he wanted to know everything about her, although he was beginning to believe that he could spend the rest of his life with her and never know all of her.

"I work part-time for a small local company that specializes in preserving and restoring old buildings," she told him as she began threading up Gloria with that night's trailer. "Hugh owns part of it. We buy up old buildings, repair them so that they look the way they did when they were new and then sell them. I'm in charge of the research, dating the structures, then scouting out replacement materials to fit each building. You wouldn't believe how badly some of the places we buy have been remodeled—or remuddled, as we call it. The company's small, only about three years old, but someday I might be able to work there full-time, if I ever leave Wheeler's.''

Hugh Kingsley again, Zachary thought, bristling. The guy seems to be everywhere, like a bad rash. "That sounds interesting," he said, watching her back as she worked. "Do you have a degree?''

He saw her spine stiffen. "You don't have to have a degree to have an interest, or an aptitude. I love what I'm doing, and I bring that love to my work. You ought to try it sometime. Maybe then you wouldn't go around the country, taking beautiful old theaters and turning them into plastic cutouts.''

I knew we had differences, Zachary thought as Sharon opened the first reel bin and practically threw a loaded reel at him, telling him to start threading up the movie, *but I didn't know they went this deep..*

''Those big old theaters were beautiful, I grant you,'' he said as he worked, ''but they're not profitable any longer. It's either cut them up into multiscreen houses, like I'm going to do with the theaters I just bought here, or close them down entirely. That's progress, Sharon, something you seem to fight at every turn.''

He stepped back from Victoria as Sharon came swiftly over to his side of the room and yelled at him, ''Progress! Then you call what they did to the Michigan Theatre in Detroit *progress*! They turned that lovely old building into a parking garage, Zachary. All that gorgeous plaster carving, and those beautiful paintings on the walls and ceilings—stripped away and mutilated as if some hungry giant had reached in his ugly fist and ripped out its heart. Is that what you call *progress*, Zachary?''

Sharon's huge blue eyes were spitting hot sparks at him, and Zachary involuntarily recoiled from the flames. He felt a momentary twinge of guilt, because he had seen before and after pictures of the Michigan, and knew she was right. And although he hadn't sold any of the theaters he'd acquired knowing that they would either be razed or, like the Michigan and so many others, raped of their beauty, he was guilty of gutting many of the theaters so that they could be rebuilt as multiscreen houses.

"Now you're letting your heart rule your head. Not every old theater can be converted into a nightclub or a symphony hall, Sharon. Some of them just have to go. The day of the big downtown theater is past. Unless the house can be updated, it'll lose all its business to the shopping mall theaters. It's too bad, but you're looking at the whole thing from only one angle."

He watched as Sharon's eyes lost their luster, as if she was somehow closing in on herself. "No one could ever accuse you of that, could they, Zachary?" she said in a small voice. "Even here, with Wheeler's, you found a way to make the place turn a profit, even if it wasn't in cash. You bought your father a little bit of happiness and salved your conscience at the same time. Not only that, but you made sure you got a little fringe benefit just for yourself, in the person of one very grateful female manager. I really have to hand it to you, Zachary. You've got more angles than Paul Newman did in *The Sting*."

"Here we go again! I thought we settled that. I told you—"

"Hey, Sharon?" Both the occupants of the room turned to look at Sheila, who was standing just inside the door, her eyes wide. "Um, sorry to interrupt. Sam says he thinks he's got a hot one in row six. Fire-engine-red compact. One patron. Sean's busy fixing a speaker pole in row two some yo-yo knocked over. You gonna check it out? Hey, what's that yellow stuff doing on the floor? You guys doing something weird? I smell paint."

Zachary looked over at Sharon, who was standing with her hands on her hips, slowly shaking her head.

"What's she talking about? It sounds like some sort of code."

Sharon looked at Gloria and Veronica, then back at Zachary. "We're ready to roll here, Sheila, so we have time. Tell Sam that Mr. St. Clair and I will handle it."

"Yeah, well, when you're done with that, maybe you'll get that Stosh fellow out of here," Sheila complained. "He keeps eating all the popcorn."

"Yes, Sheila. Thank you. I'll see to it," Sharon answered brusquely as the teenager looked at the yellow line on the floor once more and opened her mouth to ask another question, before thinking better of it and backing out of the room, slowly shaking her head.

Then, turning to Zachary, Sharon went on, "We'll leave our discussion until later, if you don't mind. Right now I think we could both use some comic relief. Follow me."

After carefully locking both doors to the projection booth, Sharon headed for the sixth row, past the teenagers sitting on the hoods of their cars, walking in between the lawn chairs set up by other patrons, and around the many spread blankets littered with small children in pajamas. Zachary spotted the small compact the same time she did, and he stopped beside her behind its rear bumper, copying her stony-faced, spread-legs, folded-arms stance.

"What are we doing?" he asked out of the corner of his mouth, trying hard to keep a stern look on his face. "I feel like a cigar store Indian standing here."

"Just shut up, and try to look menacing," she told him, pushing out her bottom lip and blowing at an

errant lock of blond hair that had fallen down over her
eyes. "Look. He's already beginning to squirm."

Zachary did as he was told, and immediately noticed that the young boy sitting behind the steering
wheel was looking decidedly uncomfortable, darting
several quick glances into his rearview mirror while
fidgeting about in his seat as if someone had slipped a
thumbtack underneath him when he wasn't looking.

Then something very strange happened. The small
car began to rock up and down, and a dull, thumping
noise drew Zachary's attention to the small trunk.
"What in hell is—"

"Shh," Sharon cautioned softly. "Now the fun
starts."

The thumping grew louder, the rocking more pro-
nounced, but the driver of the little red compact only
faced front and tried to look as if nothing out of the
ordinary was going on.

He was fighting a losing battle. Finally, first looking at Sharon and Zachary in a way that had Zachary
feeling almost sorry for the teen, the boy got out of the
car and walked back to the trunk. The moment he
turned the key in the lock the lid of the trunk flew
open.

"Holy cats, Pete, what's the matter with you anyway?" the first boy out of the trunk asked, shaking his
head. "Tony had his foot in my stomach the whole
time. Do you have any idea how big his feet are?"

"Yeah, Pete," complained the second boy as he le-
vered himself out of the trunk and onto the ground.
"Why didn't you let us out?"

"Good evening, boys," Sharon then purred, walking up to the three boys. "I hate to be the bearer of bad news, but I do believe you two gentlemen might owe me some money."

"Who's that?" one of the boys asked Pete, who was looking as if he just might become ill.

"Unfortunately for you, she happens to be the manager," Zachary supplied cheerfully, joining Sharon beside the trunk. The three boys looked up, all the way up to Zachary's face, which was nearly a full foot higher than theirs. He smiled down on them almost kindly, then said, "And me, I'm her hit man."

"I told you that you'd enjoy yourself," Sharon said, watching Zachary counting out the small mountain of change onto the worktable. "For a minute there I thought you were going to do a little *Dirty Harry*, and tell the kids to 'make your day.' I can remember Popsie doing the same thing to kids when I was little. Some things never change, and every summer teenagers try to sneak in here by hiding out in car trunks. Poor kids, with today's small cars it must be quite a squeeze."

Zachary finished counting and swept the coins off the worktable and into his hand. "We're still twenty cents short, Sharon," he told her, hefting the weight of the money, "but I think we can let it go, don't you? Lord, I thought I'd die when that kid in the trunk handed me thirty-five cents in pennies and two peppermint candies. When I used to usher at my dad's theaters we had to watch the fire exits. One kid would pay, then open the side door and let all his friends sneak in for free." He smiled and shook his head. "Funny how you forget those things, isn't it?"

Sharon looked at him, standing there holding the money out in front of him, his fascinating green eyes alight with memories. He looked so young, and so thoroughly pleased with himself. He looked, she thought as a small, sharp pain pierced her chest, so utterly lovable.

Watch it, Wheeler, her small voice warned, *you're falling right back into the same old trap. That theater he's talking about probably doesn't even exist anymore. He probably turned it into just another chrome and plastic multiscreen platter house, with no personality, no history, no beauty. Now it's nothing more than another notch in his corporate belt, another good investment. He doesn't have any finer feelings. He just uses things for his own benefit. His theaters . . . and you.*

"Yeah, well," Sharon said now, nervously looking around the small room. "It's getting dark. I've got the house trailer and cartoon ready here on Gloria. I think it's time to get the show on the road."

Zachary put the money back down on the worktable and walked over to stand beside Veronica. Tipping an imaginary hat to her, he quipped, "Ready when you are, C.B.," and turned to look out the small window at the blank screen. "Roll 'em."

Sharon ignored his antics, gave Gloria one last quick check, and then started the projector. The blank screen immediately came to life, dotted with dancing popcorn boxes, soda cups and well-dressed hot dogs. A merry tune accompanied their lively jig around the big clock face that showed there to be six minutes still remaining until show time.

The cartoon and previews for the two films to be shown at Wheeler's the next weekend followed, before a huge picture of an American flag waving in a stiff breeze appeared on the screen, while a John Philip Sousa march played over the speakers.

"You've got to be kidding. An American flag? I've been good, you know. I didn't say anything about the tap-dancing hotdogs. But this is really too much."

Sharon looked at Zachary strangely, not quite understanding his amusement. Popsie had always shown this film before the first movie. It was as much a part of Wheeler's as she was. "What's wrong with it?" she asked, too surprised to be angry. "We used to play the national anthem around the Fourth of July, but the sound finally wore out."

"The national anthem?" Zachary repeated, and she could hear the amazement in his voice. "Good Lord, woman, what did the people do when they heard it? Hop out of their cars and stand at attention?"

Drawing herself up to her full height, Sharon replied haughtily. "We're an American theater. That's the American flag. What do St. Clair's theaters run before the movie—a reminder not to throw litter in the aisles?"

"Litter's a problem," Zachary answered, a bit shamefaced, and Sharon felt a rush of satisfaction as her verbal dart hit home. "Chewing gum's the worst. We're thinking of not selling it anymore in the snack bars."

"Oh, please, stop," Sharon pleaded nastily. "You're breaking my heart. Now look lively, it's almost time to start Veronica."

She watched Zachary take his cue and then set Veronica in motion, silently admonishing herself to behave. She knew she was being mean, but she couldn't help but try to get a little of her own back for, after all, she had been listening to him tearing down Wheeler's, hadn't she? Now the score was just a bit more even.

As she broke down the house trailer reel and inserted the second reel of the movie that would pick up where Veronica left off, she tried her best not to watch what was going on over on Zachary's side of the yellow line. She had to admit to herself that he had been doing well so far, to her complete surprise, and if nothing unforeseen happened they might just get through this evening without a major catastrophe. She rather doubted it, but she hoped so.

Zachary seemed to be hoping the same thing, she decided an hour later as the final reel of the first movie was running down and the other five reels had been rewound and returned to their bins. As a matter of fact, he had been absolutely charming, bringing her a soda from the snack bar, and even helping her to pull out a stubborn carbon stick that had somehow gotten wedged too deeply into its holder.

But it wasn't until intermission that Sharon finally let her guard down completely, laughing uproariously as Zachary took over the microphone and read off the sales pitch George had written on a file card before he and Lucien had deserted them.

"Please don't forget to visit our snack bar," he read in a loud, booming voice, "where we feature freshly popped hot buttered popcorn. That's right, ladies and gentlemen, *real butter*! No artificial flavoring here at Wheeler's. And while you're at it, don't forget to check out our beef barbecue, steak sandwiches and hot dogs, as well as our wide variety of cold beverages, candy, ice cream and *delicious* nachos. My God, what a ridiculous spiel. There, how did I do?"

Sharon raced over to turn off the microphone. "That was wonderful, Zachary," she told him, giggling, "but if you don't mind a little friendly criticism, next time you might want to turn off the mike before you ask for a critique of your performance."

She watched as Zachary looked blankly down at the microphone, then at her, before his face split in an embarrassed grin. "Tell me I didn't really do that," he begged, leaning his forehead against hers.

Instantly their on-again, off-again rapport was back in full force, and Sharon gloried in the warm feeling his closeness evoked, closing her eyes and allowing herself to melt against his chest. "Shari?" she heard him say from somewhere just above her. "Do you think we'll ever stop fighting long enough to figure out what it is that's happening here? You do feel it, too, don't you?"

Slipping her arms around his waist and giving him a slight squeeze, she leaned back in his embrace and looked up into his eyes. "Oh, yes, Zachary, I feel it, too," she admitted huskily, aching for his kiss.

She watched entranced as his head slowly began to dip toward hers, and her mouth opened slightly as his lips hovered just inches above her own. Their differences faded away as she melted into a soft puddle of feelings, knowing that, on this level at least, they seemed to be of the same mind. Impatient for his touch, she moved her head slightly forward, eager to taste him, hungering to love him, oblivious to the world around them.

Chapter Ten

But the world came crashing in anyway.

"Hey, guys, would you believe it?" Sheila Bizinski called, pushing open the door from the snack bar. "This guy comes in here and says he wants me to come outside and watch the movie with him after intermission. He was kind of cute, so I took a peek outside a couple of minutes ago. Get this—he came here on a *bicycle*! Now I ask you, where does he think I'm supposed to sit—on the handlebars? Hey, guys?" she called again, stepping completely into the room. *"Whoops!"*

Sharon and Zachary sprang apart guiltily and immediately tried to look very busy, making totally unnecessary adjustments to Veronica's aperture plate. "Yes, Sheila," Sharon said inanely, not looking at the girl, "I know I forgot to speak to Stosh about eating the popcorn. I just have to finish setting up in here. Okay?''

"Sure—er—sure thing," she heard the teenager reply carefully. When she finally heard the soft closing of the door, Sharon collapsed weakly against Veronica's metal frame, totally undone.

She felt Zachary's cool lips begin to trail a hot line of kisses down her exposed throat and shivered. "At the risk of starting another argument, my dear, I believe we had discussed keeping that door locked at all times," she heard him say as his lips hovered above her left ear.

Sharon sighed before flipping the switch that would start the first reel of the feature presentation, then turned around to pull Zachary's head down to hers. "I'll say this for you, St. Clair. When you're right, you're right."

It was dark in the projection booth, and the only sounds they heard were the whir of the film as it passed through the projector and the muted bangings going on behind the door to the snack bar as the workers began to close up for the night. Standing close together, their arms around each other, their lips straining in a kiss that went a long way toward healing the wounds they had inflicted upon each other all week, Sharon and Zachary found it easy to divorce themselves from their surroundings.

As she ran her fingers through the soft curling hairs at his nape, Sharon felt as if she had been caught up in a great love story, like the ones she had watched with Popsie on the late show. Like Deborah Kerr and Burt Lancaster in *From Here to Eternity*, Sharon could believe that she and Zachary were lovers, lying together on the shore as the waves of passion rolled over them. All of her being centered on him, her very heart beat for him, her soul cried out to his, and nothing and no one else mattered.

Zachary, too, appeared to be oblivious to anything but her, feeling him drawing her closer, ever closer into his embrace, as if he could somehow meld them together into a single whole. His lean, muscled body was hard, straining against hers, and the rough, uneven tenor of his breathing sent a dizzying sense of power through her.

This time it meant something real, something honest. This time there was no denying it, no rationalizing it away. She loved him. And he loved her. She knew it, sensed it, exulted in it.

Until, from somewhere in the distance, the discordant sound of several dozen honking horns rudely shattered the moment, and sent the two of them scrambling to one of the small windows to see what was wrong.

"There's no sound," she heard Zachary whisper hoarsely before he turned away from the window and began inspecting Veronica. "There's no damn sound!"

Sharon stayed at the window a moment more, watching the actor's lips moving and hearing nothing but the impatient car horns of her disgruntled patrons. Her mind went totally, frighteningly blank. *No sound, no sound,* she chanted silently. *What do I do if there's no sound? Dammit, George, how could you do this to me!*

Zachary had already removed the covering plate from the sound box beneath the projector head, and was looking inside at the maze of wires and tubes. "What the hell do we do now?" he asked, his voice steely cold. "I don't remember the first thing about the insides of this damned museum piece."

Running over to the cabinet over the worktable, Sharon reached inside and grabbed a handful of pamphlets, scanning them quickly until she came up with the repair manual for the sound head. She paged quickly to the index, then turned to the last page and the list of troubleshooting ideas printed there.

"Zachary," she called loudly over the sound of the horns, "are all the switches on?"

"Of course they are. The thing was working a minute ago. What are you doing? The natives are getting restless out there. Hurry it up before they charge the place."

"I'm reading you the list of possible problems."

"Does it say anything there about the damn thing being too old? Veronica here should be collecting old-age benefits, not showing movies."

"Shut up and listen," Sharon ordered, quickly scanning the list in front of her. Were the speakers plugged in? What a stupid question! Of course they were plugged in. Who made up these lists, anyway— sadists? "Zachary, is a fuse or breaker blown either on the main circuit breaker or on the projection control panel?"

Zachary ran over to check the circuit breaker while Sharon opened the projector panel and scanned the interior.

"No luck here," Zachary told her before running back to Veronica. "How about the amplifier?"

Sharon checked the amplifier, sighed and picked up the pamphlet once more, while Zachary did the only other thing he could think of—he kicked Veronica right in her solid metal base.

"Ouch!" he yelled, holding his foot. "Dammit, Sharon, find something!"

"Here's a good one, Zachary!" she yelled at last. "Look inside the sound head. Is your exciter lamp burned out?"

There was a long silence, long enough for Sharon to look up from the page she was reading and see that Zachary was staring at her with a strange look in his eyes. She felt suddenly naked, as if he had inspected her from head to toe.

"It is now, Sharon," he said at last, his voice sounding defeated, and then he shut Veronica off, picked up the microphone and made an announcement. "Sorry, folks, but we've had a small mechanical problem. Please bear with us; the film will be starting up again shortly."

Still holding the open booklet in front of her, Sharon watched as Zachary removed a bulb from the sound head and replaced it with another he found underneath the worktable. Once the film was running again, she walked over to him and tentatively placed one hand on his arm.

"I'm sorry, Zachary," she said, feeling the tension in his body. "I guess I panicked. George is always here to help at times like these."

"You know, of course, that there wouldn't be times like these if Wheeler's had decent projectors?" Zachary pointed out. "Are you ready now to come out of the dark ages and admit that I'm right? How do you expect to keep customers coming back if they can't be sure of your service? Tomorrow morning I'm going to take you to one of my theaters. Then maybe you'll understand what I'm talking about. That is," he ended, moving past her to stand beside Gloria and watch for his cue to change reels, "if you think you're up to facing a little reality."

Sharon stepped back against the wall and watched Zachary work, his quick, efficient movements made even crisper by his obvious anger. She closed her eyes, wondering how everything that had been so lovely just a few minutes before could have turned to ashes so quickly.

Then, closing her eyes against the tears that threatened to fall, she remembered that Burt and Deborah hadn't had a happy ending, either.

Sharon tried her very best to dislike everything she saw late that Sunday morning at one of the St. Clair Theater Corporation's multiplex theaters Zachary took her to in a nearby town, and for a while it worked.

"Imitation butter flavor. It figures!" she scorned, after taking a bite of the popcorn Zachary offered her as they stood in the huge modern foyer of the shopping mall theater. "At Wheeler's we use real butter— and lots of it. And look at those prices! You do know that's highway robbery, don't you, Mr. St. Clair?"

"Indoor theaters have captive audiences, Sharon," Zachary told her as they walked through the foyer toward the stairs. "Operators can charge pretty much what they like. Of course, this carpeting could never survive if our menus were as varied as yours. Just popcorn, drinks and candy here, no barbecue."

As they rounded the corner and began walking down the wide hallway, she saw that there was even a second, smaller snack bar at the other end of the theater. "Just how big is this place? I've never been here."

"Nine screens," Zachary told her as he took hold of her elbow and guided her up the carpeted stairway to the second level. "We built this place when the mall went up, about five years ago. Each theater holds between 150 and 600 patrons, although we don't always have every theater open."

"That's a lot of popcorn," Sharon said in a small voice as she allowed herself to be led down a narrow hallway toward a plain tan-colored door.

Opening the door ahead of her, Zachary ushered her through to another hallway, lined with more than one hundred huge plastic bags containing popped popcorn. "No, Shari," he said, waving his arm toward the bags, "*that's* a lot of popcorn. We pop it up here in a special room, then take it downstairs as it's needed. I'd say this supply should last us about three days, two if it's busy."

"That's almost obscene," Sharon said, turning away. She'd give her eyeteeth for a new popcorn machine, but he'd never know that. But then, she thought meanly, he's never had hot coconut oil splash onto his arms as he ladled it out of the top of Wheeler's antique popper.

"Here's the projection complex, Sharon," she heard Zachary say, pride evident in his voice. "I think it's time you saw these platters you seem to think are destroying the industry."

Sharon held back a moment as Zachary used a key to open another door, then slowly walked inside, ready to hate everything she was about to see.

The first thing that struck her was the color—or the absence of color. Everything was tan—the floor, the walls, the ceiling, the projectors, even those strange three-tiered metal platters that looked like oversized pizza pans that had been stacked to look like five-foot-high avant-garde Christmas trees.

Her second reaction was to be amazed at the sheer size of the projection area. It couldn't really be called a room. It was more like a very wide hallway that ran from one end of the theater complex to the other, with projectors and tiers of pizza pans scattered together along the floor at irregular intervals.

"I feel like I'm in a submarine," she said, taking a single step forward and then stepping back again, almost afraid to move in this space-age environment. "And it's so quiet. Almost eerie."

"There are seven projectors running right now," she heard Zachary say as he nodded to the young man who walked by on his way to one of the projectors at the other end of the room. "If we didn't keep the speakers turned down in here the noise would drive the projectionist crazy."

"The projectionist? As in *one* projectionist?" Sharon asked, spreading her arms. "For all this?"

As if her question was all he was waiting for, Zachary immediately launched into a description of the ins and outs of platter houses, explaining how seven reel films were spliced into one huge reel, then laid on a platter that fed directly into the projector.

"The second platter holds the film after it comes through the projector, winding it from the outside in, so there's never a need to rewind. Once the film is done, the projectionist just threads up again and he's ready to roll. With a hit film—like *Star Wars*, for example—the film can even be run along the wall, threading through three projectors or more at once, so that the film can be shown in three theaters at the same time."

That's it? It's that simple? A well trained child could operate these machines, Sharon thought, trying hard not to look impressed. "That's very interesting," she said dully. "I'm surprised you even need a projectionist."

"There's still plenty around here for a trained projectionist to do, Sharon," Zachary answered. "The platters simply eliminate the busywork and free him up for the more important jobs."

"How perfectly wonderful. Can we go now?"

But Zachary was just getting started. To Sharon, he looked like a child showing off his classroom on parents' night. He didn't look at all like a bloodless businessman. Could it be that Zachary actually felt something deeper for the theater business than the bottom line on the annual report?

Sharon watched as he went over to one of the glassed-in windows and looked through it to the screen inside one of the theaters. "Come here, Shari. I want you to see this."

She was beginning to feel petty, beginning to question her earlier doubts about Zachary and his motives. Dragging her feet all the way, Sharon joined him at the window, allowing herself to be only slightly mollified as she felt his arm go around her shoulders, drawing her closer to him. "This movie is almost over. Now watch what happens."

The sweating, muscle-bound warrior on the screen shook his oversize machine gun at the sky, then froze into fierce immobility as the words The End rolled up from the bottom of the screen. Just as the credits disappeared, the houselights began to glow brighter, intermission music began to play, a soft light went on behind the blank screen, and the projector turned itself off. No human hands ever touched a switch.

"Magnificent, isn't it?" Zachary whispered into her ear as they backed away to make room for the projectionist, who butted his cigarette into an ashtray and then joined them beside the projector. "Now all Harry here has to do is thread up again and the entire sequence will reverse itself, lowering the houselights, stopping the music and so on. The previews and any other short films we might be showing are already spliced onto the reel, ready to go. *That*, my dear, is automation; and *that* is why Harry can run so many screens by himself."

Sharon was impressed. She would have had to be a fool not to understand how automation had improved the quality of the theater business. But that didn't mean she had to like it. "Nine theaters, one projectionist. Three, I imagine, since Harry isn't a machine and can't work twenty-four hours a day, seven days a week. Very cost-efficient. In the old days, with two projectionists to a film, it would have taken eighteen men to run nine films. Your so-called progress has put a lot of people out of work, Zachary, people like George, who lived for their jobs. *That's* what automation means to me."

Zachary grabbed her by the arm and walked her quickly down to one end of the room, away from Harry, who had begun looking at her strangely. "What are you trying to do, Sharon, incite a riot? I didn't invent automation, for crying out loud. We're trying to compete with cable television, videocassette recorders, all sorts of competition movie theaters didn't have years ago when they were the only game in town. We had to give better service, provide state-of-the-art sound systems, offer a larger variety of films or lose our audience.

"Nobody planned to put projectionists out of work. It was just a by-product of the progress we made. You know it, so why don't you take that chip off your shoulder you've been wearing ever since we came in here, and admit it?"

Sharon pursed her lips and stared at the blank wall opposite her, trying hard to ignore the truth that Zachary had pointed out to her, but it was a losing battle and she finally had to acknowledge it. "I guess Veronica and Gloria have outlived their usefulness," she said at last, trying hard to laugh. "Old projectors never die, right, Zachary? Their carbons just start drifting."

Her head jerked up as Zachary grabbed her arm and began pulling her over to the nearest projector. "No!" he fairly shouted in his excitement. "That's why I brought you here—to show you how, with a few simple changes, the old girls can go right on showing movies for the next twenty years. Look, Shari," he said, pointing to the lamp house on the projector, "that's a xenon bulb in there. We can replace the carbons with bulbs like that and, presto, Veronica and Gloria get a new lease on life. Instead of changing carbons every two reels George can change a bulb once a year."

Sharon leaned down to get a look at the bright light through the small, shielded opening. "Really?" she asked, biting her lip. "How do we do that?"

"There's a company in the Midwest that specializes in rebuilding old projectors. I called them Wednesday, and they say it can be done after this season is over." Zachary was speaking quickly now, and Sharon realized that he was nervous, worrying about her reaction to his news.

"And the platters?" She eyed him warily from her bent-over position as she asked the question. With a platter, only one projector would be needed.

"I see no reason to send George or my father into shock, do you? I think Veronica and Gloria are a great team, and I wouldn't want to break them up. Besides, if we don't keep them busy changing reels, George and Dad might start chasing the girls in the snack bar."

She straightened, turning away from the lamp house, and looked up into Zachary's beautiful green eyes. "You're a very nice man, do you know that?" she told him softly, not bothering to hide the love in her own eyes. "You had this whole thing planned, didn't you? I don't know how you stand me. I've been awful, haven't I?"

Zachary pulled her back behind the shutdown projector, out of sight of Harry. "Lady, you've been the toughest sell I've ever had," he said on a sigh as he drew her against his chest.

After lunching at a roadside café, Sharon and Zachary arrived back in Allentown just after three o'clock, then headed for one of the downtown theaters that had just become part of the St. Clair Theater Corporation.

Sharon had asked Zachary to explain the reason behind the visit, but he had been remarkably close-mouthed about it. She might have continued to push him for an explanation, but she had all she could do to contain her happiness at their new closeness, and the thought never occurred to her.

Sharon stood admiring the stucco facade of the exterior of the Regency Royale Theater, which she already knew had been built in 1925, while she waited for Zachary to unlock the door. She remembered that the theater area had been executed in the French style, complete with carved imitation-marble columns and gilt opera boxes lining the side walls. The large balcony swept out partway over the floor seats in a graceful swirl, and she could remember the times she had visited the Regency with her grandfather, the two of them paying more attention to the ornate paintings on the vaulted ceiling above their heads than on the movie being projected on the screen.

What she didn't remember, she realized as she walked inside with Zachary, was how absolutely vast the foyer of the theater was, the entire area banded on three sides by carved mahogany double staircases with a view of the separate balcony lobby and massive crystal chandeliers marching along the three-story-high ceiling. To the left of the lobby, with its leaded-glass door padlocked shut, was the old-fashioned soda fountain she and Popsie would visit after the show, to feed her grandfather's sweet tooth on cold fudge sundaes with chocolate ice cream.

Wordlessly, she followed Zachary through the doors into the main theater, and they stood halfway down the center aisle, surrounded by silence. The huge chamber was cloaked in shadows even in the daylight, and when she spoke, it was in a whisper, almost overcome with sadness. "What do you plan to do with it? Please don't tell me you're going to tear all this beauty out and put in red, white and blue plastic arches."

"Actually," Zachary responded, looking very much like Little Jack Horner about to pull out a plum, "I thought I might be able to talk you into helping me with it. I'd like to make it into a three-screen house, but I can't see any way to do it and still keep the character of the place."

Sharon felt an immediate thrill rush through her body, her mind's eye already seeing the foyer as one

small intimate theater. As for dividing the main theater into two separate rooms, well, it wouldn't be too
difficult, if she could use the balcony someway to—

She quickly applied mental brakes to her enthusi-
asm. *Here we go again,* she thought sadly, looking at
Zachary, who was smiling at her in a way that made
her feel as if all that was needed was a fat, juicy car-
rot dangling from his hand to make the picture complete.

"You want *me* to help you? Why?" she asked, eyeing him carefully. "Doesn't your corporation have
architects—whole departments—to handle things like
this? Why would you need me?"

She watched as he shook his head, a strange smile
on his face. "You still don't get it, do you, Sharon? I
guess I can't blame you, because it took me a while to
figure it out myself. I *don't* really need you to help me
with the theaters, but I think the theaters need you to
watch out for them. You love these old places. So did
I, at least until I let business get in the way of my
memories, of my real priorities. You've rekindled that
love, and I'll always be grateful to you for that. But
now, with all that I've learned, I find that there's
something still missing in my life. That something,
Sharon, is you."

Sharon closed her eyes, hardly daring to believe
what she was hearing. "Do—do you mean—"

"I mean, my darling Shari," he said softly, raising
her chin with one finger so that she was forced to look
directly into his eyes, "that I love you—very, very
much. I don't know how it happened, or when it happened, but somewhere between meeting Gertrude and

chasing you in and out of bathrooms, I have fallen madly, passionately and *eternally* in love with you.''

Sharon swallowed hard on the lump in her throat. "Oh," she said, struggling to marshal her scattered thoughts. "So now you want me to work for you?"

"No, darling," he told her, drawing her gently into the circle of his arms, "now I want you to work *with* me, *beside* me. I want you to keep my eyes open to all of the beauty and the history that mean so much to you." He lowered his head toward hers, his green eyes sparkling in the dim light. "But most of all, I want you to love me, marry me and bear my children—all that hokey stuff they used to make such beautiful movies about. Am I asking too much, Sharon? I know this is all happening very fast, that I'm rushing you, but, please, don't tell me I'm asking too much."

Sharon couldn't trust her voice, so she let her actions speak for her. Raising one hand to encircle his neck, she drew him down to her, parting her lips for his kiss.

And in the middle of the center aisle of the old Regency Royale Theater, just like in the movies, the hero won the heroine for his own, as the screen slowly faded to black.

The summer sun was just going down when the low-slung sports car pulled through the gates and drove up to stop beside the slightly crooked box office.

"Two please," the driver said, holding out a ten dollar bill, knowing there would be change. "Hold the lollipops, at least for another few months."

"What?" Sam said, hanging up the phone after telling the caller that the movie would start in half an hour. "Hey, Denny, look who's here! It's Shari and Zachary. Shari, does George know you're coming? He's just been saying that it's been a long time between visits."

"Yes, it has, hasn't it? We haven't been back to Allentown since the reopening of the Regency Royale in March," Sharon answered, smoothing the skirt of her cotton sundress over her still-flat stomach, "but I think he'll forgive us when we let him in on our little secret."

Denny leaned across Sam to say, "If you're talking about making Lucien a grandfather, Sharon, George already knows. I didn't know it was supposed to be a secret. You should have seen your father last Saturday night after you called, Zachary. He was handing out free candy bars to every customer who came into the snack bar. I told the wife, but she wasn't surprised. She said she knew you two would do just fine, seeing as how you met at Wheeler's, like we did. Now get going, you guys are holding up the line. We've got Disney tonight."

Zachary pulled the sports car ahead to the fifth row, then turned into a spot next to a vacant speaker pole. "Come on, 'wife,'" he teased, opening the car door on his side. "You've been driving me crazy asking for popcorn with *real* hot butter, so let's see if we can beat the crowd at the snack bar. Then we can check in with Dad and George in the projection room before the movie starts."

"Don't forget Gloria and Veronica, darling," Sharon reminded him. "George said they look just gorgeous with their new face-lifts." Taking Zachary's hand after he opened the door on the passenger side, Sharon stood up outside the car and looked around the theater grounds.

The bright yellow sun was hanging just above the tree line on the horizon, and a boldly striped hot-air balloon was lazily drifting by over the top of the white movie screen. All around families were settling themselves on blankets or car hoods, munching popcorn and warning their children to be careful to watch for cars as they ran to ride the brand new merry-go-round on the playground.

Zachary slid his arm around Sharon's shoulders as they walked along the gravel pathway toward the snack bar. She pressed her blond head against the side of his chest, snuggling into his familiar embrace as the two of them silently shared the heartwarming feeling of coming home.

For it was springtime, and just one more night in the seemingly endless string of nights at Wheeler's— America's oldest operating drive-in.

* * * * *

Author's Note

Shankweiler's Drive-In, located in Orefield, just outside Allentown, Pennsylvania, is America's genuine oldest operating drive-in theater, and Wheeler's Drive-In is modeled after it. Owner Susan Geissinger and her projectionist husband, Paul, were both extremely helpful, lending their knowledge and expertise to the creation of this book. In return for their graciousness, this author would like you to know two things. First, Shankweiler's is today what Wheeler's became after the St. Clairs arrived on the scene, a beautifully kept, smooth-running operation that remains a favorite summertime theater. And secondly, they serve their popcorn with real butter!

* * * * *

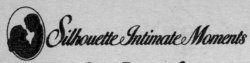

COMING NEXT MONTH

#574 WORTH THE RISK—Brittany Young
As a photojournalist, Sam Granger lived with constant danger in the Central American rain forests. But that didn't keep Francie Wilder from following him there—loving Sam was worth the risk.

#575 A DELICATE BALANCE—Arlene James
Rugged Rico Pardan wasn't fooled by Kylie Stevens's angelic appearance. His new partner was a wildcat—and nothing had prepared him for the kind of heat this lovely firebrand could generate....

#576 THE FOREVER MAN—Theresa Weir
Widow Sommer McBlain was leery of cowboys—especially handsome ones like Wade Malone. But how could she resist when his touch could gentle her skittish heart?

#577 THE TIDES OF LOVE—Elizabeth Hunter
In a single, fateful moment, Ruth Gaynor, the darling of the London stage, had been wrongly implicated in a murder. Only the love of dashing barrister Aidan Wakefield could save her....

#578 SARAH'S CHOICE—Karen Young
Sarah Carmichael thought her life was dull, but Brian Savage had always found her exciting. Could he show Sarah that he was all the adventure she would ever need?

#579 ALMOST PARADISE—Debbie Macomber
Book Three of the LEGENDARY LOVERS TRILOGY. Deep in the woods, spunky Sherry White, camp counselor to seven little geniuses, met attractive, slightly stuffy Jeff Roarke. Could she teach him how to live happily ever after?

AVAILABLE THIS MONTH:

Silhouette Romance™
Legendary Lovers Trilogy

BY DEBBIE MACOMBER....

ONCE UPON A TIME, in a land not so far away, there lived a girl, Debbie Macomber, who grew up dreaming of castles, white knights and princes on fiery steeds. Her family was an ordinary one with a mother and father and one wicked brother, who sold copies of her diary to all the boys in her junior high class.

One day, when Debbie was only nineteen, a handsome electrician drove by in a shiny black convertible. Now Debbie knew a prince when she saw one, and before long they lived in a two-bedroom cottage surrounded by a white picket fence.

As often happens when a damsel fair meets her prince charming, children followed, and soon the two-bedroom cottage became a four-bedroom castle. The kingdom flourished and prospered, and between soccer games and car pools, ballet classes and clarinet lessons, Debbie thought about love and enchantment and the magic of romance.

One day Debbie said, "What this country needs is a good fairy tale." She remembered how well her diary had sold and she dreamed again of castles, white knights and princes on fiery steeds. And so the stories of Cinderella, Beauty and the Beast, and Snow White were reborn....

Look for Debbie Macomber's *Legendary Lovers* trilogy from Silhouette Romance: *Cindy and the Prince* (January, 1988); *Some Kind of Wonderful* (March, 1988); *Almost Paradise* (May, 1988). Don't miss them!

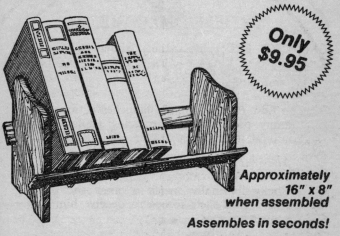

Silhouette Special Edition

NORA ROBERTS'S 50TH SILHOUETTE NOVEL

In May, SILHOUETTE SPECIAL EDITION celebrates Nora Roberts's "golden anniversary"—her 50th Silhouette novel!

The Last Honest Woman launches a three-book "family portrait" of entrancing triplet sisters. You'll fall in love with all THE O'HURLEYS!

> *The Last Honest Woman*—May
> Hardworking mother Abigail O'Hurley Rockwell finally meets a man she can trust...but she's forced to deceive him to protect her sons.
>
> *Dance to the Piper*—July
> Broadway hoofer Maddy O'Hurley easily lands a plum role, but it takes some fancy footwork to win the man of her dreams.
>
> *Skin Deep*—September
> Hollywood goddess Chantel O'Hurley remains deliberately icy...until she melts in the arms of the man she'd love to hate.

Look for THE O'HURLEYS! And join the excitement of Silhouette Special Edition!